## Killing Quick

A calm fatalism settled over Johnny Valentine. He had met brash fools like this too many times before, and he knew nothing would deter them. Every man has a limit to how many insults he can take—even Johnny Valentine. He took his stance.

Wellman, the kid in black, grinned fiendishly and spit on the floor. His hands dipped downward, but they never found their targets. Johnny Valentine's gun leaped into his hand faster than the eye could blink, and the big Colt .45 roared.

The impact of the bullet knocked Wellman back against the table where he had been sitting a few moments before. He seemed to hang there, his empty hands flung back and dangling. Then his legs gave way, and his weight went down on the table, tipping it over. Both the table and the dead gunfighter hit the floor. Danny Wellman was now just a crumpled pile of black.

**The Badge: Book 7**
**THE IMPOSTOR**

The Badge Series
Ask your bookseller for the books you have missed

# THE BADGE: BOOK 7

★

# THE IMPOSTOR

★

## Bill Reno

 TM

Created by the producers of
Stagecoach, Wagons West,
White Indian, and Winning
the West.

Book Creations Inc., Canaan, NY · Lyle Kenyon Engel, Founder

BANTAM BOOKS
TORONTO · NEW YORK · LONDON · SYDNEY · AUCKLAND

THE IMPOSTOR

*A Bantam Book / published by arrangement with
Book Creations, Inc.*

*Bantam edition / October 1988*

*Produced by Book Creations, Inc.
Lyle Kenyon Engel, Founder*

ISBN 0-553-27466-X

*Published simultaneously in the United States and Canada*

*Bantam Books are published by Bantam Books, a division of
Bantam Doubleday Dell Publishing Group, Inc. Its trademark,
consisting of the words "Bantam Books" and the portrayal
of a rooster, is Registered in U.S. Patent and Trademark Office
and in other countries. Marca Registrada. Bantam Books,
666 Fifth Avenue, New York, New York 10103.*

PRINTED IN THE UNITED STATES OF AMERICA

KR    0 9 8 7 6 5 4 3 2 1

# THE
# IMPOSTOR

## RIFLES THAT WON THE WEST

Sharps carbine

Winchester repeater

Double-barreled Shotgun

The breech-loading Sharps carbine, manufactured during the 1850's was a popular early rifle of the West, due to its accuracy and speed of firing—up to ten times in one minute.

The Winchester repeating rifle, one of the first to use metallic cartridges, quickly took over the Western market after its introduction in 1866.

Shotguns such as the double-barreled Greener were a favorite among stagecoach and bank guards and were especially prevalent in mining camps.

# Chapter One

Standing behind the desk in the small lobby of the Sunflower Hotel in the sleepy town of Medicine Lodge, Kansas, Horace Perkins made ready to begin a new day. The aging clerk unlocked his cash drawer, filled the inkwell, and, adjusting his glasses on the tip of his stubby nose, opened the register book. Dipping a pen into the inkwell, he wrote the date: June 27, 1882. Perkins applied a blotter to the wet letters, and as he lifted it, he paused and let his eyes rest on the name of the guest just above the date. It was the final entry he had made the night before: Daniel Wellman.

Perkins snorted in derision at the name. The minute that the cocky young upstart had swaggered through the lobby door just before midnight, asking for a room, the clerk had smelled trouble. Wellman had been dressed entirely in black—hat, shirt, vest, scarf, pants, and boots—no doubt trying to look fearsome and evil. The double black-leather gun belt draped over his narrow hips was gaudily decorated with studs, and even his nickel-plated Colt .44s had ebony handles. The clerk had known for certain that Wellman meant trouble when, as the

1

young man signed the register, he had boasted that he was the nephew of famous outlaw Jack Decker, and that his uncle was coming to Medicine Lodge the next day to meet him.

Anyone in a four-hundred-mile radius knew that wherever the infamous Jack Decker appeared, calamity followed. Perkins intended to pass the word on to the town marshal as soon as he had a chance. The marshal would not be too happy to learn that the infamous Jack Decker was coming to Medicine Lodge—especially since his gang would undoubtedly be with him.

The clerk twirled the end of his gray mustache as he thought about what might happen. If trouble did come, he would get out of the way in a hurry. He had not managed to reach seventy-three by being reckless, that was for certain.

Perkins laid the blotter aside and then closed the register. As he did every morning, he took his pocket watch from his waistcoat and cast a quick glance at the pendulum clock on the wall. He adjusted the hands on his watch accordingly, then looked past the faded red brocade banquette through the lobby's dusty, flyspecked window. He could tell by the light of the early-morning sun that it promised to be another hot day in Medicine Lodge. He hoped the temperature would be the only thing that would get hotter that day.

Two young cowboys, barely in their twenties, came in from the street and approached the desk, nodding at the clerk. Perkins knew both of them; Rudy Mills and Ben Ferguson were the sons of local ranchers.

"Good mornin', Mr. Perkins," Mills said.

"Howdy, boys," the elderly clerk replied cordially. "What can I do for you?"

"Did you have a fella by the name of Danny Wellman

check in yesterday?" asked Ferguson. "I got a letter from him a few days ago. Said he'd be in on the twenty-sixth."

Perkins was about to give an affirmative answer when a high-pitched male voice came from the top of the stairs.

"I sure did, you two coyotes! And I always keep my promises."

"Hey, Danny!" exclaimed Mills. Elbowing Ferguson in the ribs, he said, "Now, don't he look like a real dangerous hombre?"

Ben Ferguson laughed. "He fairly makes me tremble in my boots!"

Wellman came down the stairs with the same haughty swagger that had annoyed Horace Perkins the night before. As the cocky kid in black reached the bottom of the stairs, Ben Ferguson said dryly, "Boy, that's quite a getup, Danny."

Missing the sarcasm in his friend's voice, Wellman hooked his thumbs in his gun belt and proudly said, "Thanks, Ben. I got it four days ago in Wichita." He paused for effect, then continued, "When I became a full-fledged gunfighter."

Rudy Mills's eyebrows arched. "You killed a second man?"

"Yep," replied Wellman, bouncing on the balls of his feet. "And wait'll you hear who." Again the skinny man in black paused for effect. Finally he said with obvious pride, "J. J. Mason."

Mills and Ferguson looked at each other blankly, then subtly nodded in mutual understanding. Neither had heard of J. J. Mason, but they would not let on to their friend.

"J. J. Mason!" exclaimed Mills, feigning wonder and awe.

"J. J. Mason!" Ferguson echoed, and then turning to the clerk, who was leaning on the desktop listening to the conversation, he said, "Now ain't that somethin', Mr. Perkins?"

Horace Perkins knew he was expected to go along with the ruse, but the elderly man did not like Wellman, and he did not mind showing it. Looking Wellman over from the top of his long, stringy hair to the tips of his scuffed, black-booted feet, he gave him a sardonic stare and replied dryly, "Never heard of J. J. Mason. Must have been some fumble-fingered trail bum."

A sullen anger flashed in Wellman's pale blue eyes. He reached the desk in three strides, then sank his fingers into the old man's shirt, pulling him up close to his pock-marked face. "You tryin' to get smart with me, you old geezer?" Wellman snarled.

Horace Perkins showed no fear at all. Meeting Wellman's hard gaze, he said, "You better be careful about swaggering around and blowing off your mouth like you were some great gunfighter. You might meet up with a real one and take a six-foot drop into the ground."

Still clutching Perkins's shirt, Wellman swung a hand back, hissing, "Why, you—"

Ben Ferguson seized Wellman's wrist. "Leave him alone, Danny. C'mon, let's go set a spell and catch up."

The greenhorn gunfighter looked dully at his friend for a few seconds, then released Perkins with a shove. While Mills and Ferguson pushed him toward the door, Wellman looked back over his shoulder at the hotel clerk and warned, "If you want to live to see your next birthday, old man, you'd best watch your mouth!"

The door slammed shut behind them, and Perkins shook his head. "That young whippersnapper won't be long in this world," he mumbled to himself.

The young men sat down in three of the chairs that lined the front porch. Through the open windows Perkins heard Wellman tell his two friends that he was going to stay close to the hotel all day because his uncle would be looking for him here when he rode into town.

"Why is your uncle meeting you here in Medicine Lodge?" Ferguson asked.

"We're gonna have a talk. For a long time I've been after Uncle Jack to let me join his gang, but he's always put me off, saying I had to be old enough, tough enough, and fast enough with a gun. Well, it's been nearly a year since we last spoke, and I'm nineteen now and a lot tougher, too. Had two saloon fights last month—plus, of course, I've taken down them two men."

Ferguson wanted to ask him how old the men were that he had fought in the saloons, but he decided to let it go.

"So now I think I'm ready to join my uncle's gang. I wired him right after I killed Mason a little more than a week ago, and I told him it was time for us to talk again. He wired back and said for me to meet him here today."

While Danny Wellman continued to spout off, Horace Perkins slipped out the back of the hotel and hurried to inform the marshal that Jack Decker was coming to town. The marshal was not in his office, so the old gentleman left a note on the door.

Perkins had just let himself back into the rear door of the hotel and taken his place in the lobby when a lone rider trotted by, weaving among the wagons and buggies that moved in both directions. The rider hauled up in front of the Rusty Spur Saloon, which was directly opposite the Sunflower.

"Hey, look over there!" Rudy Mills suddenly exclaimed, pointing across the street.

A rugged-looking man eased from his saddle and wrapped the reins around the hitch rail. A revolver hung low on his left hip in a well-worn holster tied to his muscular thigh. He was over six feet tall, broad across the shoulders, and

narrow at the hips. In his early thirties, the man was
rawboned, looked as tough as boot leather, and was handsome in a roughhewn way. His shaggy, sandy hair, which
hung out from his sweat-stained, broad-brimmed hat, and
his drooping mustache were reminiscent of Wild Bill
Hickok. The rider scanned the street momentarily, and
then he ambled into the saloon.

"Wow!" gasped Rudy Mills. "It's him!"

"Who?" Ben Ferguson asked.

"Johnny Valentine!"

Danny Wellman's eyes widened, and then he punched
Mills lightly on the shoulder and said, "Hey, Rudy, don't
kid an old pal."

"I ain't kiddin', Danny. That man you just saw go into
the Rusty Spur is Johnny Valentine."

Eyeing his friend suspiciously, the young man in black
grunted, "How would you know? Johnny Valentine lives
in Texas."

"True," agreed Mills. "He's been down in Texas so
long, most folks think of him as a Texan, but he was born
right here in Kansas. I even got to see him in a gunfight
about four years ago. He looks different now. He didn't
used to have such long hair. But it's him all right."

"When did you see him in action?" asked Ferguson.

"When he took on Reed Sloan and left him dyin' in the
street with his gun still in leather."

"Reed Sloan, huh?" sneered Wellman. "I hear tell he
was pretty mediocre." An evil glint was in his eyes as he
looked across the street and added, "Maybe Johnny Valentine ain't so all-fired fast after all."

Rudy Mills stood up and looked down at his friend.
"Look, Danny, I know what you're thinkin'. You just
forget it, you hear?"

"Yeah, Danny, you'd be a fool to go against the likes of

Valentine," Ben Ferguson chimed in. "Plenty of top gunhawks have tried it, and they're all six feet under."

With his pale blue eyes fixed on the door of the Rusty Spur Saloon, Danny Wellman got to his feet. Then he spat and hitched his gun belt, determination written all over his face.

Rudy Mills grabbed his friend's arm. "Danny, listen to me. The two men you outdrew were nobodies. Ben and me, we were only pretendin' that we'd heard of J. J. Mason. We never heard his name before you spoke it! We never heard of that other guy you shot, Curly what's-his-name, either. The man over there in the saloon, Johnny Valentine, is number one, Danny. Don't be a fool."

"He ain't gonna be number one for much longer," Wellman said with a sneer. "Just think how proud my uncle Jack'll be when he rides in and hears my name on everybody's lips. His little nephew, Danny, has just out-gunned the famous Johnny Valentine. It'll be a cinch to become a member of his gang then. And I'll be a part of the most feared gang in Kansas."

While Danny Wellman's friends were trying to talk sense to him, Johnny Valentine leaned on the bar in the Rusty Spur, one foot on the brass rail, and downed a double shot of whiskey.

"Want another one, stranger?" asked the amiable bartender.

Valentine nodded, shoving the empty glass toward him.

As he refilled the glass the bartender made friendly conversation, curious to find out about his customer. "My name's Harry Boyle," he said.

"That's nice."

"In town on business?" Boyle asked, trying again.

"Just passing through."

"Been on the trail long?"

"Not too long."

"You from Oklahoma?"

"Nope. Texas."

"Headin' for Wichita?"

"Nope. Dodge City."

The laconic exchange ended when another customer called to the bartender.

Valentine drank his second whiskey slowly. After a few sips, he turned around, leaned his back against the bar, and scanned the faces of the dozen or so patrons sitting at the various tables. One by one they casually glanced back at him without recognition.

Valentine swiveled around, once again facing the bar. He had almost finished his drink when Danny Wellman swaggered through the batwing doors with his two friends on his heels.

Wellman, not wanting Johnny Valentine to be able to leave the saloon without walking past him, sat down at the table nearest the door. When his friends were seated, Wellman tipped his black hat back on his head and raised a hand, snapping a finger. "Bartender! Let's have some whiskey over here! And bring your best—ain't nothin' too good for the man who just took out J. J. Mason in a quickdraw over in Wichita!"

Harry Boyle gave the punk a sour look, picked up a bottle and three glasses, and headed for the table. The other patrons of the saloon looked disdainfully at Wellman.

Setting the bottle and glasses on the table, Boyle said to Wellman, "Not only have I never heard of this guy Mason you gunned down, but I seriously doubt that I've ever heard of you."

Wellman narrowed his eyes. "Well, mister, after today you and everybody else in this part of the world will know my name. It's Danny Wellman. Remember it. You'll speak it with reverence from now on."

Harry Boyle merely shook his head and returned to his place behind the bar.

Johnny Valentine stood with his glass in hand, observing the scene in the large mirror that hung on the wall behind the bar. He almost laughed out loud at Wellman in his all-black outfit, and he found the cocky youth's high-pitched voice an irritation. Deciding he had had quite enough of the Rusty Spur Saloon, Valentine drained the glass and set it down.

At that same instant, the irritating voice lashed out from across the room, "Hey, you at the bar! You're the famous Johnny Valentine, ain't you?"

Boyle's head whipped around as he stopped in mid-swipe with his bar rag. Every eye in the saloon stared at the customer at the bar. Valentine's name was known throughout the territory, even if his face was not.

Valentine focused on Wellman in the mirror. The kid was now standing away from the table, his feet spread apart. Without bothering to turn around, Valentine answered blandly, "Yep, Johnny Valentine is my name, all right. As to the 'famous' part, well, I'll leave that to others to decide."

Wellman's eyes were fiery as he said with a sneer, "Well, Valentine, I'm itchin' to find out if you're as fast as they say."

Valentine looked at his young challenger's reflection in the mirror and said, "You don't really want to know, boy."

Wellman bristled. "I ain't no boy—and I assure you that I do want to know!" he snapped.

The experienced gunfighter continued to eye Wellman in the mirror. Then he replied wearily, "Do yourself a favor, kid, and go home. Don't go out of your way to look for trouble—or to start something you'll regret."

But Wellman persisted with his taunting remarks.

Pivoting around slowly, Valentine just stared for a moment at the skinny figure standing before him. Finally, in a grating voice, he said, "Kid, you can make this saloon your graveyard if you want to, but why die when you're so young? And you *will* die, 'cause you can't outdraw me. Think about it, kid. You'll never again hear the birds sing in the morning. Never taste the sweet lips of a pretty girl. Never smell the honeysuckle on the night air. I'll say it again, kid. Go home. Because I'll kill you if you go after that gun."

Wellman looked the tall man up and down, a wicked leer curling his thin lips. "I guess you're all talk, huh?"

Valentine's hazel eyes glinted coldly, and he said angrily, "If you're itching to face me in a shoot-out, wait a few years and grow up first."

Rudy Mills grabbed his friend's elbow. "Danny, give it up. The man's trying not to have to kill you. Don't you see that?"

Shrugging off his friend's hand, Wellman bellowed over his shoulder, "Shut up, Rudy! I know what I'm doin'!"

"Your friend is giving you some sound advice, kid," Valentine said icily. "Better listen to him."

Wellman's face turned redder. "You won't draw against me because you're just a gutless coward. Now I know how you've stayed on top so long. You were able to talk other men out of a showdown 'cause they were even bigger cowards. Well, I ain't gonna back down, Valentine, so say your prayers!"

A calm fatalism settled over Johnny Valentine. He had met brash fools like this too many times before, and he knew nothing would deter them. They would have their big moment, no matter how senseless it was.

Sighing, Valentine took his stance. "Okay, kid, you're getting your wish. Too bad it will be your last."

The kid in black grinned fiendishly. Every man has a

limit as to how many insults he can take—even Johnny Valentine.

Wellman's friends leaped from their chairs to get out of the line of fire, and the other patrons did the same. From Valentine's left, Harry Boyle said timidly, "Mr. Valentine, I wonder if you'd mind moving outside. That mirror behind you cost a great deal of money."

Without looking at the bartender Valentine replied, "Don't worry about it. Sonny boy won't even get his guns out of their holsters."

Wellman spit on the floor and held splayed hands over the ebony handles of his Colt .44s. Breathing heavily with excitement, he said, "We'll see about that, Valentine! Draw!"

A predatory look replaced the placid one on Johnny Valentine's face. With a caustic edge to his voice he countered, "This is *your* big moment, kid. *You* draw."

Wellman's hands dipped downward, but they never found their targets.

Johnny Valentine's gun leaped into his hand faster than the eye could blink, and the big Colt .45 roared.

The impact of the bullet knocked Danny Wellman back against the table where he had been sitting a few moments before. He seemed to hang there, his empty hands flung back and dangling. Then his legs gave way, and his weight went down on the table, tipping it over. Both the table and the dead gunfighter hit the floor. Danny Wellman was now just a crumpled pile of black.

Valentine holstered his smoking gun as the bartender breathed a sigh of relief, grateful that his mirror was still intact.

While Ben Ferguson hovered over Wellman's body, Rudy Mills stepped up to the gunfighter and said, "Mr. Valentine, have you ever heard of Jack Decker?"

"Who hasn't?" Valentine shifted his gaze from the huddled black form to the face of the young cowboy.

"I think you ought to know that Danny Wellman was Jack Decker's nephew."

Valentine raised his eyebrows in surprise.

"Decker's on his way here right now to meet Danny," said Mills. "Don't get me wrong, Mr. Valentine. I'm not tryin' to tell you what to do. But when Decker finds out you killed his nephew, he'll probably turn his whole gang loose on you. So you might want to make tracks for someplace safe."

Valentine knew Rudy Mills was right. Jack Decker would be after him with a vengeance for killing his nephew, and he could not take on the whole Decker gang by himself. "Thanks for the information, kid," he said, and he made a quick exit.

As he rode out of town at a gallop, Valentine realized that the bartender and the patrons in the saloon had heard him say he was headed for Dodge City. With that information Jack Decker would have no trouble following him. Since Valentine had business to take care of in Junction City as well as Dodge, he decided to head there first. When Decker reached Dodge City and found no trace of him, the gang leader would have no other leads to follow. By the time Valentine arrived in Dodge, Decker and his bloody gang would have given up the chase and headed elsewhere.

Smiling to himself, Johnny Valentine clucked at his mount, guiding him northeast toward Junction City.

While riding through the now vaguely familiar Kansas territory, the gunfighter recalled the years that he, his parents, his brother, and his sister had lived in Dodge City. Most of his memories were happy ones; the saddest was remembering how he had broken his parents' hearts when he ran away from home at fifteen during the Civil

War, to join William Clarke Quantrill and his band of raiders loyal to the Confederacy.

Quantrill had been operating out of Kansas and Missouri, making sporadic raids on Union troops that had occupied Missouri after 1862. Johnny Valentine had joined the band as a wide-eyed idealist, but he had soon been disillusioned after witnessing one particularly bloodthirsty raid.

In August 1863, Quantrill and four hundred and fifty of his men swooped into Lawrence, Kansas, shooting every man and boy in sight before burning the entire town. The young Valentine had been sickened by the savagery of his fellow raiders. He quit Quantrill's Raiders near the war's end, ready to go back home and start rebuilding his life, only to find that, unlike regular soldiers, the guerrillas were denied amnesty. Johnny Valentine was suddenly an outlaw.

Figuring they were considered outlaws anyway, some of his fellow recruits—such as Frank James and his brother, Jesse—had taken the guerrilla tactics they learned from Quantrill and applied them to robbing banks and trains.

But Valentine had put his abilities to a different use. While with the guerrillas, he had been drilled relentlessly in marksmanship. Now he took that skill from town to town, sometimes using it to win big wagers, other times hiring himself out as a guard to stage companies carrying large payrolls—warding off robberies by his former fellow guerrillas.

It did not take long before someone decided to put his marksmanship to the test, challenging Valentine to a shootout. Since that time, he had learned how to talk a lot of men out of the attempt—but not nearly enough, as far as he was concerned.

When the statute of limitations finally ran out and he was no longer considered an outlaw, he thought he would be able to go home and settle down into a normal life. But his reputation followed him, making it impossible for him to live quietly as he had hoped. He was able, however, to return home and make things right with his family, and it was comforting now to know that when his parents had died, two years before, it was with their oldest son back in their good graces.

He had been away far too long, and now he was eager to see his sister in Junction City and his brother in Dodge.

Valentine rode until dark and then stopped for the night. The next day he continued, and at noon he stopped in Hutchinson to rest his mount and eat a midday meal. Leaving the horse at a nearby stable, he walked up Main Street and entered a small café.

Threading his way among the tables to an unoccupied one, he sat down. He was just settling in his chair when he became aware of a short, stocky form looming over him. Valentine looked up, and his eyes settled on a familiar face. Smiling broadly, Valentine stood up, extending his hand. "Charlie Buttons! How are you?"

"Just fine, Johnny," said the shorter man, grinning. "Haven't seen you in a coon's age. Last I knew you were in Texas."

"Have you eaten?" queried Valentine.

"Nope. I followed you through the door. Didn't know it was you till I studied your face for a moment."

"Time does take its toll, doesn't it? Well, sit down and let's eat together. It'll be just like old times, Charlie."

They gave the waitress their orders, and she returned with two steaming mugs of coffee. Valentine studied the face of his old friend for a moment, and then he smiled and said, "Well, Charlie, are you living here in Hutchinson now?"

Buttons sipped his coffee before replying. "Yeah. I've still got relatives in Dodge, but Mary and I moved to this town seven years ago. I own the hardware store and gun shop."

Johnny nodded. "Doesn't surprise me. Same business your dad was in all those years you lived in Dodge. Everything going okay?"

"Couldn't be better. But tell me, what are you doing back here in Kansas?"

"Well, you probably know that my sister, Emma, moved to Junction City when she got married."

"Mmm-hmm." Buttons nodded. "I hear she got a divorce not long ago."

"Yeah," said Valentine sadly. "She's still living there, though. And my brother, Jim, is still living in Dodge, of course."

Charlie grinned. "That little brother of yours will never pull up his roots, Johnny. He'll live and die right there."

"I'm sure of it. Anyway, you know our parents are both gone now."

"Yes, I did hear that some time back. I'm sorry."

"Thanks. It took quite a while to settle the estate because my dad had holdings in several places across Kansas. I got a letter from Emma about three weeks ago, and she told me that the money's in a bank in Abilene. I have to get signed documents from both Jim and Emma and then take them to their attorney in Abilene to collect my third of the inheritance."

"Well, I'm sure glad you've come through Hutchinson," Charlie said with a grin. "It really is good to see you again."

"Same here."

"Too bad about Emma's divorce," mused Buttons. "Has she got a new man in her life yet?"

"As a matter of fact, she does. In the same letter, she told me she's been seeing a man named Frank Lane for about a year now. Must be wedding bells in the offing.

She said in the letter that his business keeps him traveling some, but she hopes he'll be in town when I come. Wants him to meet me. Ah! Here's our food," Valentine suddenly exclaimed. "Good. I'm starved. It's been a long, hard day."

When Johnny Valentine rode out of Hutchinson an hour later, his plan was to pace his horse and ride most of the night, stopping periodically along the way and taking quick naps. That way he would arrive in Junction City in time to have his breakfast with Emma.

# Chapter Two

**"W**hat do you mean, he's dead?" shouted Jack Decker at the top of his voice. His lips were pulled back over his teeth like those of a rabid dog.

Horace Perkins's face was chalky white as he stood nose-to-nose with the outlaw leader. "H-he was killed in a quick-draw g-gunfight, Mr. Decker," the elderly desk clerk explained nervously to the small, wiry man with a black patch over his eye.

Decker stepped away and began to pace with a slight limp. His frown was so much a part of him that it seemed likely the outlaw had not smiled since he was a child—if he had even smiled then. He had lost his left eye in a saloon brawl years before, and visible in his remaining coal-black eye was an evil ruthlessness.

Three of Decker's four men were still astride their horses outside the Sunflower Hotel. Watching Decker was his lieutenant and bodyguard, Hunt Longley, who stood six-feet-seven in his socks, weighed nearly three hundred pounds, and was as mean as a grizzly bear with four sore paws. But he followed Decker around like a puppy, and like all the men in the gang, he jumped when Decker spoke and did as Decker ordered.

The outlaw leader suddenly stopped pacing and leaned over the clerk's desk, seizing the old man's shirt. Viciously snapping Perkins's neck, he hissed, "When did this happen?"

"Not more than t-two hours ago, Mr. Decker," answered the terrified Perkins.

"Who did it?"

"Mr. Decker," choked out Perkins, "it happened at the Rusty Spur Saloon, r-right across the s-street. Why don't you go talk to the bartender? He saw it firsthand. I didn't."

"I'll talk to him when I'm good and ready!" growled Decker. "I asked you who gunned down my nephew!"

"I . . . I would rather not say, Mr. Decker," gasped the elderly clerk, blinking nervously. "He might come back and—"

Decker let go of the man's shirt and backed up two steps. Motioning to his huge bodyguard, he said, "Tear his face off, Hunt."

As Hunt Longley moved toward him Horace Perkins stammered, "N-no! I'll . . . I'll tell you. It was . . . it was Johnny Valentine."

*"Johnny Valentine!"* Decker pounded a fist into the palm of the other hand. "So Valentine's stooped to killin' kids, eh? Well, we're goin' after him, Hunt. I'm gonna kill him myself."

Longley's deep bass voice sounded as though it were coming from the bottom of a well. "Boss, you ain't gonna brace Valentine in a draw are you?"

"Naw, I ain't stupid," replied Decker, looking up at the towering monster. "You boys are going to get him in a corner so I can cut him to pieces an inch at a time—and laugh while I'm doin' it. Come on. Let's go see what we can find out from the bartender."

A few minutes later, Decker and his gang barreled into the Rusty Spur. The outlaws were like vicious dogs, snarling and ready to attack and kill at their master's command, and the patrons watched and waited fearfully.

The wiry man with the patch over his eye leaned over the bar and growled at the bartender, "Why didn't you do something to stop it?"

"S-stop what, sir?"

"Stop the murder of my nephew, that's what!" Decker roared.

"Excuse me, sir, b-but I'm not sure I know what you're talking about."

"There was a gunfight in here earlier, right? And Johnny Valentine murdered a kid named Danny Wellman. Now, don't tell me you could forget a cold-blooded act like that so fast, barkeep."

Harry Boyle gulped nervously. Watching the huge man who stood next to Decker from the corner of his eye, he replied shakily, "Wh-what do you think I could have done about it, Mr. Decker? Your nephew pushed Johnny Valentine to the limit. Valentine tried to get the kid to back off. Even the kid's friends tried to keep him from challenging Valentine."

Decker's one eye gleamed with fury as he howled, "You're lyin' through your teeth, barkeep! Danny was a sensible kid. He wouldn't just up and challenge a man with Valentine's reputation! Naw, the truth is, Valentine was hungry for blood. He probably hadn't killed anybody in a day or so and just had to spill some blood. Well, he spilled the wrong blood today. Danny's blood and mine are the same. I'm gonna kill that murderous fiend if it's the last thing I do!"

"Mr. Decker," said Boyle, "you've got it wrong. It didn't happen like th—"

The bartender's words were cut off as Jack Decker's open hand lashed him across the mouth. "Don't you lie to me!" exploded the outlaw. "Danny's dead, and you could have prevented it!"

With shaky fingers touching his smarting mouth, Boyle asked, "How could I have prevented it?"

"You've got a shotgun behind that bar, don't you?" rasped Decker. "All barkeeps stash a shotgun behind the bar."

"Well, yes, but I—"

Extending a hand, the outlaw leader said, "Gimme the shotgun!"

A sense of disaster rose up in Harry Boyle. Eyes wide, he shook his head and said, "Please, no, Mr. Decker. I don't want any trouble. I just—"

Turning to his massive bodyguard, Decker barked, "Hunt, go back there and get it."

The huge bodyguard stomped behind the bar and picked up the double-barreled twelve-gauge shotgun. Sweat beaded Harry Boyle's brow, and his customers sat frozen in their chairs.

Holding out his hand, Jack Decker said, "Gimme the shotgun, Hunt."

As Decker took the weapon from Longley, Boyle said, "Please, Mr. Decker. I tell you, there was nothing I could do to keep your nephew from getting killed. He brought it on himself."

"You could have stopped it by shootin' Valentine, barkeep. Or don't you know how to use this gun? Here, let me show you."

Thumbing back both hammers, Decker swung the barrels in line with Boyle's face, and the bartender's eyes bulged with terror. His jaw slacked, and his breath came in short, jerky gasps.

Decker's finger pressed tightly against the forward-most trigger. Just before he squeezed, he swung the shotgun to aim it beyond Boyle's head. The big gun boomed, and the mirror behind the bar shattered with glass flying in every direction.

Harry Boyle emitted a tiny whimper.

Decker eyed him sternly and said, "Where'd that child-killer go when he left?"

"H-he said he was going to Dodge City."

"Did he say that before or after he murdered Danny?"

"Before."

Just then a stocky man wearing a badge on his chest bowled his way through the batwing doors and demanded, "What's goin' on in here?"

Jack Decker pivoted and gave the marshal an odious look. Bringing the shotgun around to bear on the lawman, he answered coldly, "We're killin' lawmen!" Then he squeezed the rear trigger on the twelve gauge, and once again the shotgun roared. Medicine Lodge's town marshal took the blast in the middle of his chest. The impact slammed him back through the batwings, and he landed outside on the boardwalk, dead. The badge that had glinted on his chest seconds before was gone.

Decker threw the shotgun on the floor and calmly walked through the cloud of acrid smoke that hung in the saloon. "Let's go, boys," he said. The gang filed back outside, stepping over the marshal, and mounted their horses.

Decker reasoned that since Johnny Valentine had told the bartender where he was going before Danny was killed, he had probably changed his destination after the shooting. Valentine was from Texas; he must have come north for some reason, so he would not immediately head south again. That left either east or north, since Dodge City was to the west. Jabbing spurs into their horses' sides, the Decker gang galloped out of Medicine Lodge.

As luck would have it, Decker chose to lead his men in the same direction Johnny Valentine had taken a few hours earlier.

The dew-laden fields of wheat surrounding Junction City, Kansas, sparkled like diamonds in the early-morning

sunlight as Johnny Valentine passed through them on his
way into town.

He rode slowly down Main Street, looking around at the
few people who were stirring, and guessed that it was
probably around seven o'clock. Passing by the Butterfield
Overland Mail Company office, he watched the stagecoach crew loading the luggage rack on top with cargo.

A block farther, Valentine turned off Main Street and
rode the two short blocks to his sister's house. He had only
been to Emma's house twice—the last time five years
before—but it was all as familiar to him as if he had been
there yesterday. Emma would no doubt be up and preparing breakfast just about now, and his mouth watered at
the thought.

Dismounting in front of her house, Valentine stepped
up on the porch and rapped on the door. When there was
no response, he knocked harder. Still there was no answer. He made his way around to the back of the house,
thinking that Emma might be at the privy.

"Emma? Emma, are you in there?" he asked. He hesitated, then knocked on the wooden door. But he got no
response.

Scratching his head, he turned and walked toward the
rear of the house. He climbed onto the back porch and
knocked again. Nothing.

Valentine wondered if Emma had already married Frank
Lane, and they had moved elsewhere. Of course, she
would have written him, but the letter might have arrived
after he left Texas. He peered in through the window in
the back door. There was no sign of life in the kitchen.

Hearing a door close at the house next to Emma's,
Valentine looked over in that direction and saw a middle-
aged woman descending her steps. She waved as she
walked toward him.

"Who are you looking for?" she asked suspiciously, peering intently at Valentine.

"Emma Bowman," replied Valentine, stepping off the porch to meet her. "I'm her brother. Has she moved?"

"Not unless she did so in the middle of the night," the woman responded with a chuckle, relaxing her caution. "We had tea together yesterday afternoon, and then I noticed her lights go out around eleven o'clock last night. I doubt that she's still asleep. Emma's always up by now." A thought struck the woman, and she said, "You know, maybe she left early to go somewhere with that Frank fella she's been seeing. He's always riding the stage in and out of here. Maybe they're going off someplace together."

"I noticed the stage loading up when I rode in," said Valentine. "What time does it leave?"

"Eight-fifteen."

"What time is it now, do you know?"

"About seven-twenty."

Johnny thanked her and headed again to the front of the house as the woman returned next door and disappeared through her back door. Worry was scratching at his mind. It did not seem likely that Emma would leave town, knowing he was coming soon. He looked up at the second floor of her house and wondered if she was sick. The shades were pulled on the bedroom windows. Again, the gunfighter stepped onto the front porch, this time peering through the lace curtains covering the parlor window. What he saw sent a cold wave of shock through his body, and he stiffened. His sister was lying on the floor in her robe . . . and the robe was soaked with blood!

He grabbed hold of the knob and tried it. To his surprise, it came open, and he ran inside. There was a pool of fresh blood around Emma's body. It was even matted in her long, dark hair. She had been stabbed several times, and the long-bladed butcher knife lay beside her.

Gasping her name, he knelt beside his sister and lifted her up, carrying her over to the sofa. He gently propped her head on a pillow, and then he knelt down next to her and took her hands in his.

She began to stir. Her eyes fluttered open, and she appeared to be focusing on his face. Her brow furrowed, and she cried weakly, "Please, Frank . . . Don't kill me! Oh, please don't kill me!"

"Emma," her brother said softly, "it's Johnny. It's Johnny."

A tiny wail escaped her pale lips as his words penetrated the fog in her mind. "Johnny!" she breathed. "Oh, Johnny, you're here! Thank God, you're here! He tried to kill me!"

Valentine swallowed hard. "Emma, did Frank Lane do this?"

"Yes . . . Frank Lane, the man . . . I was going to marry. He stabbed me!"

"I know, honey. I saw the knife." The distraught Valentine eyed the bloody robe and said, "I've got to get a doctor here right away. You're bleeding bad."

Emma's face pinched. "Don't leave me, Johnny. Please, don't leave me!"

"It'll only be for a minute, Emma," he said, attempting to keep his voice level. "I'll run next door and have your neighbor go for a doctor."

Though his sister still pleaded with him not to leave her, Valentine insisted, and he ran next door and told the neighbor about his grisly discovery. Then he dashed back to his sister's side.

With what little strength she had left, Emma gripped her brother's arms when he sat down beside her, and she asked, "Please, Johnny, you won't leave me again, will you? Promise me?"

"No, Emma, I won't go anywhere. Don't worry. The

doctor will be here soon." He smoothed away damp strands of hair that had fallen into her eyes. "Emma, tell me what happened between you and Frank."

Grimacing with pain, Emma Bowman spoke with difficulty. "Frank . . . Frank played me for a fool, Johnny. For a whole year . . . he's played me for a fool. I . . . I found out a few weeks ago . . . that he's married. He has a home in Great Bend. When I told him I knew about his wife, he said he'd get a divorce and marry me. He said . . . his marriage was unhappy. But . . . but then he began to waver. This morning he came by to tell me that there would be no divorce. He . . . he explained that the money used to finance his business isn't his own but comes from his wife, Suzanne. He said she's always been his . . . his source of money, and that a divorce was completely out of the question."

Emma took a deep breath and gritted her teeth.

"Maybe you'd better not talk anymore, Emma. Wait until after the doctor has fixed you up."

"No," she breathed, "I . . . I don't think I'm going to . . . make it, Johnny. I must tell you. Frank . . . Frank wanted us to carry on like we had been. It . . . it made me angry, and I told him . . . I told him if he didn't get a divorce immediately, I would go to Suzanne and tell her about us. That's . . . when he grabbed the knife. We were in the kitchen. I ran into the parlor, trying to get out the front door, but he . . . he caught me and stabbed me, Johnny. He stabbed me! Then he ran away, thinking I was dead."

The gunfighter could feel the wrath creeping up his spine. Through his clenched teeth he said, "Where can I find him, Emma?"

"He . . . he'll be on the stage for Great Bend."

"The one that leaves at eight-fifteen?"

"Yes, but . . . please . . . please don't leave me, Johnny! Please!"

Valentine looked at the old grandfather clock in the corner of the room. It was seven forty-seven. He wanted to dash out and catch Frank Lane before the stage left, but he would not leave his sister. He swore angrily to himself. Where was the doctor? It seemed like an hour since he had sent that woman for him.

Emma's fingers were digging into his forearms. "Johnny!" she cried out. "I . . . I don't want to die alone! Johnny!" Her body stiffened. "Hold me. Johnny, please hold me!"

Johnny Valentine choked back his tears as he bent down and folded his sister into his arms. She made a gurgling noise, and he recognized the sound. It was the death rattle.

She gasped for breath and said, "Johnny . . . I . . . love you." Her voice trailed off as she spoke the words, and her body went limp.

Valentine held his sister's dead body in his arms for several moments, then laid her down gently. He climbed the stairs to her bedroom and pulled the coverlet from the bed. Returning to the parlor, he solemnly folded her arms over her breast and covered his sister with the spread. Just before he pulled it over her ashen face, he said shakily, "I love you, too, Emma. And I want you to know that the man who did this to you is going to pay. With his life."

Fury boiled up in Johnny Valentine as he bolted out the front door of the house. He swung into the saddle just as a buggy came bounding up in a cloud of dust.

The doctor reined his horse to a halt and leaped from the buggy, his eyes on Valentine. The look on the mounted man's face caused the young physician to pause.

"My sister is dead, Doctor," Valentine said coldly. "Please go on in. I'll be back shortly. I have some important business to take care of."

*      *      *

Frank Lane stood on the boardwalk in front of the Butterfield office and watched the stage crew load on the last pieces of luggage. Then he rechecked his pocket watch. It was five minutes before eight. The well-dressed businessman in his late thirties was clearly fidgety, toying with his necktie as he spoke to the Butterfield agent standing beside him.

"Edgar, can't you get these two apes to load any faster? I've got business to attend to in Great Bend—and *I* can't get there on time if this *stage* doesn't leave on time."

Bill Dixon, the driver, and Larry Elkins, the shotgunner, cast hot glances at Lane, then continued their task.

"Mr. Lane," said the agent, "the stage isn't due to leave until eight-fifteen. They'll have it loaded in plenty of time. If the scheduled passengers are here once the luggage is loaded, maybe I'll let it leave a little early. Right now, I would appreciate it if you would not annoy the crew."

Lane swore under his breath and paced back and forth on the boardwalk. He lit up a cigar, puffed on it for a few minutes, and then swearing again, threw it into the street, where it lay smoking.

At four minutes after eight, the Butterfield agent announced that the passengers could now board the stage, which would be leaving five minutes early.

"Well, it's about time!" grunted Lane, heading for the coach along with two other men and their wives, all of whom would be passengers on the trip.

When Lane stepped in front of one of the women about to board, her husband glared at him and in an icy voice said, "The ladies will get on first, sir!"

Lane halted, noted that the man was quite muscular, and stepped back. He said weakly, "Oh, uh . . . sorry." Up in the box, the driver and the shotgunner looked at each other and smirked.

Lane waited while the two husbands climbed in after

their wives. He was about to board the coach when a sharp voice pierced the morning air.

"Hold it, driver!"

Everyone on the stage, the agent on the boardwalk, even the people in the street, stopped and turned at the ferociousness of the command.

Bill Dixon held the reins taut, looking at the rugged man sliding down off his saddle. He waited for the tall stranger to speak again.

"You've got a passenger on your stage named Frank Lane!" Valentine shouted, leaving his horse in the middle of the street and walking toward the vehicle. "I want him!"

Frank Lane paused at the door of the coach and turned to look at the man who had just spoken his name.

The driver pointed down at Lane and said, "That's him right there, mister. Whatever your business is, make it quick. We're due to pull out right now."

His rage festering, the gunfighter glared at the man who had murdered his sister and bellowed, "We have a score to settle, Lane!"

Frank Lane felt the man's fury directed at him, but he felt safe with plenty of people around, and standing his ground, he gave the stranger an insolent look. "You can go to blazes, whoever you are. I don't have any business with you."

"My name's Johnny Valentine," came the gunfighter's simple reply.

Valentine's name was passed from person to person along the broad, sunlit street. Bill Dixon looked wide-eyed at his shotgunner, and Elkins shook his head and whispered, "I ain't interferin'!"

"You bet you ain't!" whispered the driver in return.

The wealthy businessman's face had blanched. He knew the name well. His heart was pounding as he swallowed with difficulty. With a tremor in his voice he asked, "What do you want with me?"

Valentine's strident voice lashed through the warm morning air. "You and I are going to have a shoot-out, Lane! You're going to draw against me!"

"Well . . . Mr. Valentine," said Lane, holding open his expensive coat to show that there was no gun belt strapped to his waist, "as you can see, I don't wear a gun, so I can't very well draw against you. And you didn't answer my question. What do you want with me?"

The gunfighter said coldly, "I've got an extra gun in my saddlebags, with holster, belt, and all. I'll be glad to loan them to you."

Frank Lane licked his lips and ran a shaky hand across his sweaty face. "I'm no gunfighter, Valentine. I'm not going to draw against you. And I don't understand. You and I don't even know each other. I can't imagine what it is you think I may have done to you. Really," he said, forcing a laugh and looking incredulously at everyone gathered around, "can any of you imagine what I could possibly have in common with this man?"

Through clenched teeth Valentine hissed, "My sister, Emma, is what we have in common, Lane."

Shock registered in Lane's eyes, and he blurted, "But how—?"

"When I found her, she wasn't dead, and she lived long enough to tell me the whole story. I guess you didn't figure on anyone finding her so fast—or maybe you thought she was already dead when you left."

Lane was thinking fast. He would surely die if he let the famous gunfighter force him into a shoot-out. Licking his lips again, he threw up his hands. "I'm not drawing against you, Valentine. You . . . you just call the sheriff in on this. Turn me over to him. I'll stand trial, but I'm not drawing against you."

"No dice," the gunfighter said stiffly. "Judges and juries can be bought. I'm not a murderer like you are, so I'm giving you a chance. Think of it this way, Lane. I'm giving you the opportunity to take me down, so I won't be able to tell your wife what Emma was going to tell her. Drawing against me is the only chance you've got to keep your marriage—and the source of all your money—from going dry."

The fire in Johnny Valentine's piercing eyes told Frank Lane the gunfighter was not bluffing. Lane thought fast. He had but one chance, and he would take it. "All right." He nodded. "You leave me no choice. Get your extra gun. I'll draw against you."

Valentine pivoted and walked toward his horse. When his back was fully turned, Lane's hand snaked inside his coat and came out with a .38 revolver.

A male voice in the crowd cut the air. "Lane's gonna shoot!"

The seasoned gunfighter's Colt was out with lightning speed as he wheeled around and fired.

The bullet slammed Frank Lane dead-center in the chest. He grunted and raised up on his toes as the slug hit him, and the .38 in his hand discharged harmlessly. Frank Lane was dead before he toppled facedown into the dust.

As the crowd began gathering around the dead man, Johnny Valentine holstered his smoking gun, adjusted his hat, and mounted his horse. He was riding away slowly when one of the male passengers in the stagecoach shouted, "Where's the sheriff? Somebody get the sheriff! Hurry up! That killer is getting away!"

Bill Dixon was climbing down from the box. Looking inside the coach, he snapped, "Johnny killed him square, mister. We all saw it. Lane was gonna shoot him in the back."

"That's right," came a voice from the crowd, and others chimed in with their agreement.

"Sounds to me like the man must have killed Johnny's sister, whoever she is," another said. "He sure didn't deny it. Johnny had good reason to come after him."

"Who is this Johnny Valentine, anyhow?" asked the male passenger who had yelled for the sheriff.

Dixon squinted at him. "You must be an easterner, mister. Everyone in these parts knows about Johnny Valentine. He's the fastest hombre with a gun this side of the wide Missouri!"

The driver sighed and turned to his shotgunner. "I guess we'd better see to the late Mr. Lane." They climbed down off the stage and found a length of canvas in which to wrap Frank Lane's limp body. Then they lifted the bundle onto the top of the coach to take to his widow in Great Bend.

When the stagecoach finally rolled out of Junction City, the shotgunner turned to the driver and said, "Bill, what are we going to tell Mrs. Lane when we bring in her dead husband?"

"You mean about the conversation between him and Valentine?"

"That's exactly what I mean."

The driver shook his head. "Sounded like some real nasty personal stuff. Ain't none of our business, and I don't want to get mixed up in it. We'll just tell her that Johnny Valentine rode up, stopped the stage, and challenged her husband. Her husband seemed to know what it was about and agreed to face off with Valentine. Then we'll just tell her exactly what happened from there. We don't know all the facts, anyway. If she wants to know more, let her find Valentine."

Larry Elkins agreed, and the matter was settled. The two men then concentrated on their job—getting their passengers safely and comfortably to Abilene, the first stop on their journey to Great Bend.

*        *        *

Valentine was making arrangements with the under-taker for Emma's burial when a group of riders thundered into town. Looking out through the window of the funeral parlor, the gunfighter saw the rough-looking bunch ride past, and he heard someone on the street holler, "It's the Jack Decker gang!"

Valentine swore to himself. Somehow the gang had picked up his trail, stayed on his heels, and followed him to Junction City. Paying the undertaker quickly, he dashed out onto the street and leaped into his saddle. Casting a cautious glance back at the riders, he saw them haul up in front of a saloon and start inside.

Spurring his horse, he rode quickly to Emma's house, went in, and searched her desk until he found the docu-ment that he had originally come to town for. Folding the paper and carefully placing it in his saddlebag, he leaped back onto his horse and rode out of Junction City, heading due south.

He was hoping to make it appear that he was on a beeline for Texas. Obviously someone in the Decker gang had an uncanny knack for tracking a man, and Valentine knew they would soon learn he had left town and would once again be hot on his trail.

He had to throw them off. Once that was done, he could head west for Dodge City to see his brother. Jim was going to be devastated at the news of Emma's murder, but Johnny had one consolation. At least he could tell Jim he had killed the man who did it.

# Chapter Three

Suzanne Lane arose from her bed the following morning and donned the robe that she had draped over the foot of the bed the night before. Pulling the bell cord for her maid, she stretched and returned to the bed to wait. A few minutes later a young servant entered carrying the usual breakfast tray and set it down on a small table in front of a bow window. Suzanne dismissed the maid and crossed the thickly carpeted floor.

She finished the light meal quickly. Then she got up and walked over to the imported French dressing table and sat down in front of the mirror. She picked up her silver hairbrush, but then she paused and said aloud to her reflection, "Everyone says that you're a beautiful and young-looking twenty-nine, Suzanne Lane. But your beauty is going to fade quickly if things between you and your husband don't improve."

The ugly thoughts were assaulting her again. What was happening to their marriage? When she and Frank were wed seven years ago, he was so thoughtful and attentive. But for the past several years, he hardly—

Suzanne shook her head. *No*, she told herself. *It isn't*

*that at all. It's the pressures of the business, that's all.
Everything will be like it was, when some of the pressures
ease up for Frank.* Fixing her mind on happier things,
Suzanne brushed her long auburn hair vigorously for several minutes, then worked it adeptly into a chignon and
pinned it at the nape of her neck. Wetting the tips of her
fingers with her tongue, she pushed some stray strands
into place. Then she turned her head from side to side as
she looked in the mirror.

*Frank has always liked my hair best this way,* Suzanne
thought. She decided not to wear a hat. This way he could
see her hair better.

After applying her face powder and adorning her ears
with a pair of gold earrings, she put on a white linen dress
that emphasized her feminine charms. She touched up her
hair one more time before leaving her room and going
downstairs.

Carrying an unopened parasol with one hand and her
purse with the other, Suzanne Lane left her house and
walked the four blocks to Great Bend's main street. Nearly
everyone in town was familiar to her, and she greeted
passersby with a smile. Men eyed her appreciatively, noting how her deep-red hair shone in the morning sun.

She reached the Butterfield stage office just after ten
o'clock. The stage was due in at ten-twenty.

Stepping inside the office, Suzanne smiled at the gangly
agent, whose unruly shock of blond hair had, as usual,
defied all efforts of comb and brush. "Good morning,
Eddie!" she chirped. "Is the stage going to be on time as
far as you know?"

Eddie Fitch gazed at the captivating woman and smiled
in return. In his mid-thirties and unmarried, Fitch often
wondered what it would be like to have such an enchant-
ing woman for a wife. Answering her question, he said,
"Yes, Mrs. Lane, as far as I know."

He stood there letting his eyes drink in her beauty. She stood about five-feet-five inches tall, and her dress accentuated her slender yet curvaceous frame. Her green eyes could be both soft and warm, but when she was angry, they could flash with a fire likely to melt the subject of her wrath.

Suzanne's features were so beautifully sculpted, they reminded Eddie Fitch of a Greek goddess he had once seen illustrated in a book. As he continued to gaze at her, he was thinking what a lucky man Frank Lane was.

Suzanne felt the force of his eyes and looked herself over, saying, "Is there something wrong, Eddie? You seem to be staring at me."

Blinking as if coming out of a trance, the agent said, "Oh, no, Mrs. Lane. There's nothing wrong at all. I was just . . . well, I . . . I was just admiring that dress, ma'am. It certainly is beautiful."

Smiling warmly, she said, "Why, thank you, Eddie." Turning toward the door, she called over her shoulder, "It's such a lovely morning, I think I'll wait outside for the stage."

The redhead stepped onto the boardwalk and took a seat on a bench near the door of the Butterfield office. Wagons, buggies, and men on horseback moved past her, going in both directions. As people passed by, Suzanne greeted them with a cheerful word and sometimes engaged in brief conversation with them.

She looked over at the clock on the town hall, and once again she thought about Frank. She wondered what mood he would be in when he arrived; he had been quite irritable and out of sorts of late. Suzanne had tried to get him to talk about what was disturbing him, and a couple of times it seemed he was going to do so, but then he had withdrawn again.

Suzanne presumed it had to do with their business

enterprises. It was extremely demanding on him, spending every other week away from home, overseeing the chain of seven general stores that were located in seven different towns across Kansas.

Suzanne, whose inherited money had enabled them to buy the stores, always kept a keen eye on the financial records. It was clear that each store was making them a good profit and was in good running order. Consequently she attributed Frank's foul moods and disinterest to his being weary from the long stagecoach rides every other week.

However, the voice in the back of Suzanne's mind told her she was trying to fool herself, and that there was something else behind Frank's disinterest in her. Their marriage was not a marriage anymore—it had become more like a business proposition—and Frank was cool and distant. Matters had deteriorated so much between them that twice, in the last month, she had confronted Frank when he returned home from trips and flatly asked him if there was another woman. But he had merely laughed and told her there could never be another woman for him. Both times he had warmed up a little and had taken her in his arms, assuring her she was the only woman he loved.

Suzanne had convinced herself to believe him, telling herself that everything was going to be all right between them, but his interest had lasted only briefly before he again retreated into his shell. Still, she felt confident that her husband was telling the truth about his fidelity.

Yet as she sat there on the bench waiting for his return, she sensed that Frank's attitude had nothing to do with pressure or weariness. And although she still loved her husband, she had to admit that she was not at all happy.

Suzanne looked up at the town-hall clock again. It was ten-thirty. The stage was late now, but then it seldom came in right on the minute. There was no cause for alarm.

Twenty more minutes passed. Worry began to scratch at the edges of her mind. Passengers waiting to board the stage were milling around, becoming fidgety and talking among themselves about the tardiness of the stage.

Suzanne decided to ask Eddie Fitch about the situation, but just as she stood up, the rumble of hooves reached her ears.

"Here comes the stage!" someone on the street called out.

The coach rounded a corner a block away, and Suzanne's heart quickened its pace. She was always excited to see her husband, even though their marriage was not as it had been. She assured herself that this time matters would be settled between them before he traveled again, and the happiness that had once been hers would be found again.

The horses snorted and blew as the stage came to a halt in front of the Butterfield office. Suzanne worked a smile onto her face; she wanted Frank to see her at her best. She looked at the driver and the shotgunner and waved. The two men lifted their hands in weak response, but neither smiled back at her. This was unlike them, Suzanne thought. She wondered if their dismal mood had anything to do with the stage being a half hour late.

Bill Dixon wrapped the reins around the brake handle and spoke to Larry Elkins from the side of his mouth. "I was hoping that for some reason Mrs. Lane wouldn't be here to greet her husband this time. It's times like this that I really hate my job."

"Yeah," Elkins said, and nodded. "Me, too."

Eddie Fitch emerged through the office door. Looking up at the driver and shotgunner, he smiled and asked sarcastically, "Well, fellows, did you stop to enjoy the scenery or something?"

As the two men climbed down from the box, Bill Dixon

replied, "One of the lead horses threw a shoe about ten miles back, Eddie. It took us a while to get it nailed back on."

Fitch noticed the sober look on their faces. "Hey, look," he said with a laugh, "I ain't really upset. I was only kiddin'."

The passengers were alighting from the coach. Suzanne Lane stood back a few feet, her eyes fixed on the coach door. When the last passenger had stepped out, the red-head waited a few seconds before taking two steps forward.

Climbing down from the box, Larry Elkins hurried to the back of the stage and lifted open the rear boot. Then he began handing passengers their luggage.

Eddie Fitch waited for the rope that secured the luggage and cargo on the top rack to be untied so he could climb up and start handing it down.

Dixon looked at the agent and started slowly untying the rope. He had dreaded this moment the entire trip. From the corner of his eye he watched Suzanne Lane peering in through the open door of the coach, consternation wrinkling her pretty brow.

When Suzanne found the coach empty, she stepped back and looked up at the driver. "Bill," she said, "did my husband perhaps get word to you why he didn't come on this trip?"

Elkins was at the rear of the coach, pretending not to hear.

Dixon let go of his rope, flicked a sober look at the back at his shotgunner, then looked at Suzanne and replied, "Ma'am . . . I . . . uh . . . I don't exactly know how to tell you this . . . but . . . but Frank *did* come on this trip."

Suzanne's brow furrowed again, and then she set her green eyes on the driver and said somewhat impatiently, "I've been here since you pulled in, Bill. Mr. Lane did *not* get off this stage. What do you mean he came on this trip? Where is he?"

Bill Dixon removed his hat, ran a sleeve across his sweat-beaded face, and said grimly, "He's up on top, Mrs. Lane. I don't know how to tell you this, but your, uh . . . your husband is dead."

Suzanne's gaze swerved to the rack. For the first time she took note of the form wrapped in canvas. Her face lost color, and her knees started to give way.

Eddie Fitch caught Suzanne and, gripping her by the elbows, assisted her to the bench where she had been sitting earlier. Fitch then called to his clerk, sitting at her desk. "Mrs. Beyers, would you please bring a cup of water? Mrs. Lane has had a terrible shock."

A few moments later Mrs. Beyers came over with a tin cup of water and gave it to Suzanne.

"I think perhaps it would be a good idea if you run and ask Dr. Chambers to come over here, if you don't mind, Mrs. Beyers," the Butterfield agent said.

"Not at all, Mr. Fitch. I'll be as quick as I can."

The young man briefly left Suzanne's side to speak to his crewmen. "Why don't you boys go ahead and take Mr. Lane's body down from the rack?" he said softly. "You can tell us what happened after Doc Chambers gets here."

"Sure thing, Eddie," the driver agreed.

Word was being passed up and down the street that Frank Lane was dead, and that his body had just been brought in on the stage. The crowd began to grow larger.

Dr. Howard Chambers, black bag in hand, was just arriving at the Butterfield office as Dixon and Elkins laid Frank Lane's body on the boardwalk and folded back the canvas covering him.

Suzanne rose shakily from the bench and walked in a daze to her husband's lifeless form. Kneeling beside him, she began to weep. "Frank . . . Oh, Frank! This can't be real. Frank, you can't be dead!"

Dr. Chambers took hold of Suzanne's shoulders and

spoke soothingly. "Mrs. Lane, come. Let me take you inside the stage office."

Tears flowed freely down her cheeks as Suzanne looked up into the physician's face and sobbed, "Oh, Doctor, he can't be dead! He just *can't* be! This can't be happening!"

"Come, my dear," he said. "I'll give you something to calm your nerves."

Giving in to his guiding hands, Suzanne stood up. She looked over her shoulder at her husband's body as Chambers led her inside.

Sitting her down, the physician mixed a mild dosage of sedative powders with water and made her drink it. While she was doing so, Eddie Fitch sent someone for the undertaker, and then he asked the driver and the shotgunner to come into the office.

Chambers was seated beside Suzanne, speaking soothingly to her, when Dixon and Elkins came in. The agent closed the door in order to give Suzanne some privacy from the crowd. Dixon and Elkins pulled up chairs in front of the window and sat down.

With harried eyes, Suzanne looked back and forth between them and asked, "What . . . happened? How did my husband die? Did he have a heart seizure?"

The two men adjusted themselves uneasily on their chairs and glanced furtively at each other.

"Well, ma'am," said Bill Dixon, "the fact is he was killed. Shot."

Suzanne gasped. "Shot? How? Why?"

Dixon told her what had happened, recounting the exact sequence of events as they had happened and the exact words that had been exchanged by the two men—but omitting all references to Johnny Valentine's sister, Emma. He and Larry Elkins had remained firm in their resolve not to tell her that her husband's death had been the result of his affair with another woman; Suzanne Lane's grief was severe enough without that bit of news.

"How do you know the man was Johnny Valentine?" asked Suzanne.

The driver answered her, "Because, ma'am, Valentine told your husband who he was. There's no question the man was Valentine. I've heard descriptions of him, and the way he got his gun out and killed Frank . . . Well, I have no doubt he was the genuine article."

"None whatsoever," added Larry Elkins.

Suzanne stared at them, wide-eyed. "You mean Valentine just whipped out his gun and cut my husband down? That's murder! Nothing but cold-blooded murder!"

"No, ma'am, it wasn't like that at all," Dixon said, shaking his head. "Valentine was sure hot about somethin', and your husband . . . well, ma'am, he definitely knew what Valentine was furious about, and he didn't put up no argument."

Suzanne's normally pink face was ashen. "Did . . . did Valentine elaborate?"

Again the two men cast each other quick glances. Shaking his head, Dixon replied, "Not really, ma'am. He just told your husband that they were goin' to square off and shoot it out."

"That was when Frank showed him he wasn't wearin' a gun," said Elkins, "and then . . . Well, that's when it happened. When Valentine turned to get the spare gun from his saddlebag, your husband pulled a .38 from inside his coat. He was gonna shoot Valentine in the back, but somebody in the crowd hollered, and Valentine shot Frank through the heart."

Suzanne's mouth was trembling. She put a hand against it, bent her head down, and broke into tears. When she pulled herself together, she said, "The sheriff should be told. They need to form a posse and go after that murdering gunfighter."

"The law won't do anything to Valentine, ma'am," said

Dixon. "Since he was aimin' to square off with Frank face-to-face, and Frank tried to shoot him in the back, the law says he's committed no crime."

Suzanne dug her fingers into her hair and wept harder, shaking her head in disbelief.

From his vest pocket Larry Elkins pulled out the .38 revolver. "This is your husband's gun," he said, handing it to Suzanne. "His other personal effects are . . . are still on his person." Elkins looked solemnly at the new widow for a moment, and then he and Dixon walked over and stood by the agent's desk.

Suzanne's head came up. In a mixture of sorrow and fury she said, "Frank didn't have a chance against a man like Johnny Valentine, and Valentine must have known it. Making Frank draw against him was nothing short of murder. Frank's only chance was to do what he did. As far as I'm concerned, the fiend murdered my husband! I can't believe the law doesn't look upon this outrage the same way!"

The four men in the room stood in silence as the beautiful redhead wept uncontrollably. Finally she drew a shuddering breath and asked plaintively, "What could that horrible gunfighter have had against Frank? What could Frank possibly have done to make Johnny Valentine want to kill him?"

Larry Elkins sighed and said, "Guess the only way to know, ma'am, would be to find Valentine and ask him personally."

A hint of fire crept into the widow's green eyes. Through clenched teeth she said coldly, "I may do just that."

The next day Suzanne Lane stood beside her husband's fresh grave amid the somber tombstones of Great Bend's cemetery. She was dressed in black with a thin-netted veil over her face. Her eyes were swollen from weeping, but as the minister was closing the graveside service with prayer, her heart was filled with rage. Suzanne did not even hear the minister's words. The fury within had her thoughts racing.

Silently the widow vowed to find the man who had taken her husband from her. Once he had answered the question of why he had killed Frank Lane, the great Johnny Valentine would die at her hand. Killing him would not be difficult. He would never expect it from a woman.

Beneath the veil, Suzanne Lane smiled to herself. The shame of having been killed by a woman would hang over the famous gunfighter's own grave forever.

When the service was over, townspeople passed by slowly to give the widow their condolences. When the last one was gone, the minister walked her to the funeral coach. He spoke quiet, tender words of encouragement, then helped Suzanne into the vehicle. The undertaker drove her directly home.

Suzanne walked into the house, closed the door behind her, and leaned against it, relieved that the ordeal was over and she was alone. She had given her maid a few weeks off, for she did not want to have to converse with anyone. Fighting for composure, she inhaled deeply and let her breath out slowly. A flush rose on her cheeks, and her hands clenched into quivering fists. "Somehow, Mr. Valentine," she muttered aloud, shaking her head, "I'm going to see that justice is done!"

Suzanne leaned against the door until the mixture of anger and sorrow had cooled. Removing her hat and veil, she moved slowly through the house to her bedroom, where she crossed to the dresser. She opened the top drawer and picked up Frank's revolver, then carried the gun over to the bed and sat down, trying to unscramble her racing thoughts.

She regretted that she and Frank had not been getting

along. Frank had seemed more deeply married to the business than he had been to her. Recently, during an argument, she had reminded him that it was her inherited money that had put him in business, and he had promised to be more attentive.

But even though they had been having their difficulties, Suzanne had been sure that in time she and Frank would have worked things out. Now it could never happen. That killer, Johnny Valentine, had taken her husband from her.

Again the wrath welled up within her. Looking down at the gun in her hands, she knew what she had to do. The gunfighter was going to pay for killing Frank; he was going to pay with his life. "If it's the last thing I ever do, Johnny Valentine," she said aloud, "I'm going to put you in your grave!"

Within a few days, Suzanne Lane had hired a man to manage her chain of stores. She was greatly relieved to have this off her mind, for now she had all her time free to accomplish her plan.

The following morning, she drove her buggy to a secluded spot outside of town. Setting up an old pair of Frank's boots on a natural mound as targets, she took the revolver from her purse and stood some ten feet away. Raising the weapon with her right hand, she sighted in and fired. The bullet dug into the ground six feet behind her target. Licking her lips, she thumbed back the hammer and took aim again, bringing the muzzle a little higher. The gun bucked and roared in her hands, and the bullet chewed dirt between the two boots.

She practiced for the rest of the morning, stopped long enough to eat the picnic lunch she had packed, and then practiced some more. She was pleased to see that her aim was growing truer. When she finally returned to the buggy, she reloaded the gun and dropped it into her purse. As she climbed in and took hold of the reins, she told herself she was ready to achieve her goal.

Her next step was to locate the famous gunfighter. She would keep her identity a secret and get to know him. If she had to, she would even use her looks and femininity as a ploy. One way or another, she would get Valentine in a corner under the muzzle of her gun and make him tell her why he had killed Frank. Once she knew the reason, she would kill him.

As the buggy rolled toward town, Suzanne's conscience stung her. A voice inside her said, *Suzanne Lane! A lady of your breeding planning a murder! What would your family think, God rest their souls?*

A sheen of sweat moistened her brow. She pulled the buggy to a halt and dabbed at her face with a handkerchief. "It's not murder," she said aloud. "It's an execution! The law won't do anything to Valentine for murdering Frank, so it's up to me. It's an execution that has to be done. That beast used his gun to take my husband from me. It's only right that I take his life from him!"

Suzanne angrily shook the reins and clucked at her horse to get moving again. As she rode back home, she thought of the irony of it: Valentine would be killed by Frank's widow, with Frank's own gun!

Nursing her hatred, the vengeful widow stopped in town and bought a ticket from Eddie Fitch for the next stagecoach to Junction City. She let Fitch think she was going there to check on her store, but her real reason for the trip had nothing to do with business; she wanted to begin her search for Johnny Valentine from the spot where he had gunned down her husband.

# Chapter Four

Johnny Valentine neared the town of Newton some seventy miles south of Junction City. He had been pushing his horse hard, and the animal was in need of a good feeding and a long rest before it could be ridden any farther.

Valentine's plan was to ride south the twenty-five or thirty miles more it would take to get to Wichita, and then make sure he was seen there, pointedly telling some of the residents that he was headed through Oklahoma back to Texas. Once that was done, he would cross the Arkansas River and ride due west toward Dodge City. He hoped the ruse would keep the Jack Decker gang going south.

The lowering sun was casting long shadows in the street when Valentine walked his winded horse into Newton. Figuring it would have taken Decker and his men an hour or so to learn which way he had ridden out of Junction City, Valentine decided to leave his horse at the livery for oats, hay, and water, and at the same time get himself a meal. After that he planned to ride out of town ahead of Decker and stop under cover of darkness somewhere on the prairie for the night.

Valentine pulled up in front of Newton's livery stable and swung stiffly from the saddle, noting that the corral was well stocked with horses. Fastening the reins to the hitch rail, he entered the barn.

A skinny young man in bib overalls was cleaning some tack. He looked at Valentine and drawled, "Howdy, stranger. What can we do for you?"

Valentine smiled and asked, "Do I detect a Texas accent?"

"You sure do," the young man said with a chuckle. "We're from down Burleson way. D'you know whereabouts that is?"

"Yep. Just south of Fort Worth."

"You from Texas?"

"You might say that," replied Valentine, pressing a little accent into his words.

"Well, put 'er there," said the youth, extending his right hand. "My name's Danny Ward."

At that moment the back door of the barn opened, and an older version of Danny Ward entered. The youth turned around and said, "Hey, Pa. This here feller's from Texas, too." Turning back to the gunfighter, Danny Ward said, "This here's my pa, Luke Ward. I didn't catch your name, sir—"

"I already know his name," the older man cut in brusquely. "It's Johnny Valentine."

The gunfighter blinked at the livery owner's hostile tone and asked, "Have we met, sir?"

"No," Luke Ward said curtly, coming up to Valentine and staring at him coldly. "But I've seen you in action a few times."

Danny's eyes were bulging as he stared at Valentine. Working his tongue loose, he said, "You . . . you're Johnny Valentine?"

"I was the last time I looked in the mirror," Valentine said with a slight grin.

"*The* Johnny Valentine, the gunfighter?"

"I'm afraid so, Danny," Valentine said wearily.

Danny Ward swallowed hard while his father said, "What can we do for you, Valentine?"

"I'm heading back to Texas," replied the gunfighter. "Need to get myself a meal and keep riding. I'd like to have my horse walked around to cool him off, then let him gobble some feed."

"Consider it done," responded Luke Ward. "He'll be ready whenever you return for him. I don't cotton to gunfighters, and I'd just as soon you leave our town before there's any trouble."

Valentine headed for the door, then stopped and said, "If it means anything to you, Mr. Ward, I try to avoid trouble whenever I can. Too bad other people don't feel the same way—they seem to *look* for it. And too often they expect me to give them what they're looking for."

Somewhat mollified, Ward called after him, "The best place to eat is the Chuck Wagon Café. Just a block to your left."

"I'll find it," Valentine said over his shoulder. "Thanks."

Danny Ward waited until his father had led Valentine's horse away. Then he ran down the street as fast as he could go. Dashing into the Driftwood Saloon, he looked around the smoky room for a few seconds, then spotted the man he was looking for sitting at a table against the back wall. Weaving his way through the milling patrons, he reached the table and said excitedly, "Charlie, have I got news for you."

Charlie Lund was in the middle of a poker game with three other men. Looking up at young Danny Ward with annoyance, he said impatiently, "Not now, Danny. Can't you see I'm busy?"

"You won't be when you hear what I got to tell you!" declared the skinny youth. "Remember how you were sayin' last week that you'd like to get another chance to go up against Johnny Valentine?"

"Seems I recollect sayin' somethin' like that," replied Lund offhandedly, studying the cards he had been dealt. "Why?"

"He's in town right now. Rode in a few minutes ago. Left his horse for Pa to feed."

Eyeing Danny with doubt, Lund said, "Johnny Valentine, the gunfighter, just rode into Newton, Kansas, and deposited his animal with your pa?"

Young Ward nodded in response.

Lund threw his cards down on the table and stood up. He adjusted the gun belt on his hips, then pulled the big iron from its holster and broke it open. Carefully he checked the loads, then eased the revolver back into the leather sheath, testing the thong that tied the holster to his right leg.

One of the men at the table said, "Why don't you play your hand before you go, Charlie?"

"Huh?"

The man said dryly, "If you're goin' out there to brace Johnny Valentine, you won't be back. We'd like for you to play out this hand so's we can win some more drink money from you."

Lund sneered at him insolently and said, "You just keep your seat, Tom. I'll be back in two shakes of a lamb's tail."

"Dead lambs don't shake their tails," the man said evenly.

Ignoring him, Lund asked Danny, "Where is he?"

"At the Chuck Wagon."

"Okay," Lund said, and grinned at his friend broadly. "I'll wait for him to come out. At least he can die with a full stomach."

Thirty minutes after he had entered the Chuck Wagon Café, Johnny Valentine emerged into the twilight. He was

surprised to see a large crowd of men gathered in the
street and arrayed on the boardwalk. He was about to
turn and head for the livery stable when he heard his
name called sharply. Looking around, he saw Charlie
Lund standing spread-legged in the middle of the street,
his right hand splayed over his holstered gun. Bystanders
were clustered on both sides of the street, and Johnny
Valentine heard his name being whispered among them.
Then he caught sight of Danny Ward in the crowd, excitement written all over the youth's face.

Valentine looked back at Lund, who had a murderous
gleam in his eyes, and he knew what was expected of him.

Valentine stepped off the wooden sidewalk, loosening
the gun in his holster. "Haven't seen you since that day in
Del Rio, Lund," he said levelly. "I didn't think I'd be
seeing you again."

"You ain't backin' me down this time, Valentine," snapped
Lund. "I've been in a lot of draws since then—and I'm still
standing."

"I always back 'em down if I can, Lund," came Valentine's slow words. "I only kill a man when he forces me to
do it."

"Well, you've killed your last man," growled Lund. "It's
your turn to die."

Valentine's hazel eyes were as cold as ice. Clenching his
jaw, he rasped, "Go for your gun, Lund, and we'll see
whose day it is to die."

Lund's hand dipped and his fingers closed around the
gun, whipping it from its holster. He was bringing it to
bear, thumbing back the hammer, when Johnny Valentine's Colt .45 roared. The jolt of the bullet hitting Lund
sent him reeling backward. He staggered a few steps, then
fell flat on his back, the unfired gun in his hand. He lay in
the street, gasping, as a crimson spot grew larger on his
shirtfront.

Valentine dropped his smoking revolver into his holster and walked over to the dying man.

Lund coughed as he looked up with hate-filled eyes at the victor, who was standing over him. Gutshot, Lund was racked with pain from his mortal wound. Coughing again, he grunted, "Well, why don't you . . . put a bullet in my head, and . . . and finish me off?"

"I beat you to the draw, Lund," Valentine said. "You'll have to do your own dying." With that, he pivoted and walked away.

The gunfighter looked straight ahead, ignoring all the staring passersby during the short walk back to the livery stable.

"Well, Mr. Valentine," Luke Ward said, leading the gunfighter's horse out by his bridle, "I guess I owe you an apology. I watched you just now, and you did your best to avoid that shoot-out." Shaking his head, he said, "Maybe Danny'll realize now that there's nothing glorious about gunfighting, 'cause there was no glory in the way Charlie Lund died." He smiled and added, "For a minute there I wasn't sure whether this handsome gelding was gonna get a new owner."

Valentine patted the animal's head. "Too often some fool out there's wondering more or less the same thing—only it's not my horse he's looking to acquire. It's my reputation."

He mounted up and extended his hand down to Ward. "Thanks for looking after my horse so well. We might even make it as far as the Oklahoma border before calling it a night."

"It was my pleasure, Mr. Valentine. Now I've got something to tell my grandchildren some day."

The heads of all the patrons turned as the shapely redhead entered the Buckhorn Saloon in Junction City, Kansas. Along with every other man in the place, the middle-aged bartender eyed Suzanne Lane with appreciation but wondered why a woman of her station would be seen inside a saloon.

Walking up to the bar, Suzanne said to the balding, heavyset bartender, "Good afternoon. I just arrived on the stagecoach, and I need some information."

"I'll supply it if I can, ma'am," the man said with a sincere smile.

"I understand Johnny Valentine was in Junction City recently."

"Yes, ma'am. Just a few days ago."

"But he left?"

"Yes, ma'am," the bartender said, and nodded, pulling the towel from his beefy shoulder and wiping the bar by habit. "Valentine gunned down the owner of our general store—a man named Frank Lane—and rode out before the gun smoke had drifted away. At least that's what they tell me. I didn't see the incident myself."

At the sound of Frank's name on the man's lips, Suzanne felt a cold numbness wash over her.

"You a friend of Valentine's, ma'am?" queried the bartender.

"Uh . . . uh, no," she replied, blinking her eyes. "I'm . . . uh . . . I'm attempting to locate him because I have some very important business to discuss with him. Actually, I've never even seen Mr. Valentine. Do you know what he looks like?"

"Not really, ma'am. Valentine was from these parts, as you may have heard, but he hadn't been back for years— until a few days ago, that is." Looking around at the men in the saloon who were gawking at the beautiful woman, the bartender asked, "Were any of you fellas on the street the other day when Valentine killed Lane?"

Suzanne inwardly shuddered at the unintentional callousness of the bartender's words, and she fought to hide her feelings.

Three men who were seated at tables and two who were standing at the bar announced that they had seen the gunfight.

"Well, this here lady needs a description of Valentine. She's looking for him."

The man nearest to Suzanne at the bar, a tall, slender cowboy, removed his hat and smiled. He moved close to the widow and said, "Johnny Valentine is about my size, ma'am, and rugged lookin'. He has light-brownish hair, and he wears it sorta long. Kind of like Wild Bill Hickok—everybody's seen pictures of him. He wears a heavy mustache like Wild Bill, too. He's real distinctive lookin', that's for sure."

Suzanne smiled at the cowboy and said, "Thank you. You've been a real help."

"Mean lookin'!" cut in another man, drawing near. "Real mean lookin', ma'am."

Facing the newcomer, she asked, "Do you mean that he's ugly?"

"Well, not exactly, ma'am. I, uh—"

"Not at all," cut in the cowboy who had spoken first. "Johnny might even qualify as handsome to some eyes. I think what Charlie means is that when Johnny came after Frank Lane, he was lookin' pretty mean. There was real fire in his eyes."

Suzanne felt her throat constrict. Swallowing hard, she nodded. Clearing her throat, she said, "Do any of you men know which way Mr. Valentine went when he left Junction City?"

An elderly man sitting at one of the tables said, "I think he went south, ma'am. Yesterday I was talkin' to a friend of mine who lives at the southern edge of town, and he told me that he saw a man of Valentine's description ridin' south out of town only a few minutes after the shootin' incident. You can talk to my friend yourself if you want to." Pausing a moment, he grinned and added, "I'll be glad to personally escort you to his place."

Suzanne gave the man a friendly smile. "Uh . . . that's all right. I can find your friend's house myself. How far is it?"

"Only about a half a mile from here. Just go left out the door and keep headin' down the street. You can't miss it. The porch is about to fall off the house—or maybe it's the house that's about to fall from the porch. Anyhow, it's on the right side of the road as you head south. Last house before you hit open country."

Suzanne thanked the men for their help and then left the saloon. She opened her parasol to shade her from the hot sun and slowly made her way on foot to the southern edge of town until she reached a house that fit the description.

As she neared it she saw an old man sitting in a rocking chair on a rickety porch.

Squinting at the lovely woman approaching him, he gallantly stood up and removed his hat, as well as taking his long-dead pipe from between his teeth. Hobbling to the edge of the porch, he said, "Howdy, little lady. What're you doin' out in the hot sun?"

"I'm trying to obtain some information," Suzanne said with a smile, standing in the dusty road. "A friend of yours said you might be able to help me."

"Yeah? Well, I'd like to do whatever I can for you, you pretty young thing. And I don't mind tellin' you that right now I wish I was forty years younger!"

Suzanne blushed.

Cackling, the old man rubbed his wrinkled face and said, "My name's Wally, honey. Come on up here on the porch and set a spell."

Suzanne did not trust the rickety porch—nor, for all his

advanced years, did she feel she could trust Wally. Smiling, she replied, "Thank you, but I've been traveling by stage for quite some time, so I prefer to stand. But please, I wouldn't mind if you sit. I just need to ask you a few questions."

"Fire away, honey," Wally said, and he sat down heavily in his chair.

"I understand you saw a man leaving town just after the gunfight the other day. Is that right?"

"Right as rain."

"Can you tell me what he looked like?"

The old man gave her a detailed description of the rider—and it was Johnny Valentine, all right. Suzanne was certain of it. She started planning her next move.

"I also seen a band of tough-looking riders headin' the same way about an hour later. They seemed to be in a real hurry," Wally continued.

"Hmm? Oh, I'm sorry, Wally, I wasn't listening. Did you say something else about Valentine?"

"Nope, about some other fellas—nasty lookin', they was."

"Well, thank you very much for all your help. I really appreciate it."

"Anytime, little lady. Anytime." The old man sighed as he watched Suzanne Lane's retreating figure head back toward the center of town.

Suzanne, using her maiden name of Stanwood, took a room at the hotel, where she planned to get a good night's rest before taking the stage to Wichita the next morning.

It was nearly evening by the time the stagecoach pulled into Newton, some twenty miles north of Wichita. When Suzanne and her fellow passengers alighted to stretch their legs and visit the privies, Suzanne noticed a group of men clustered nearby. Wanting to make sure she was still on the right track, she approached them.

"Excuse me, gentlemen, I wonder if you can help me."

She was immediately answered by one of the group, a handsome, well-dressed man. "It would be my pleasure, ma'am, to help you. Just tell me how I might be of assistance."

Suzanne blushed slightly, then said, "I wonder if, to your knowledge, the famous gunfighter Johnny Valentine has passed through Newton."

"And what would a woman like yourself be wanting with a gunfighter?" the man asked.

Suzanne had devised a logical story, and now she was telling it to anyone who inquired. "Well, you see, I am a reporter with a newspaper back in Kansas City—the Kansas City *Sun*, perhaps you've heard of it?" she asked ingenuously, then continued, "We are doing a series of articles about famous and infamous Kansans. Needless to say, Mr. Valentine is one of the representatives of the latter category. I'm trying to find him with the hope that perhaps he will agree to tell me his story." Suzanne Lane did not know the first thing about being a reporter and prayed that none of the men would question her too closely about her work.

"You're on the right track, ma'am," the man assured her. "It seems that luck is on your side—which is more than I can say for a fellow named Charlie Lund. Two days ago, your Mr. Valentine was in a shoot-out with Lund and gunned him down handily. Why, he rode out of here without even waiting to find out whether Lund had expired."

*That seems to be Valentine's pattern*, Suzanne thought bitterly to herself. *That's exactly what he did when he shot Frank*. Aloud, she asked, "Do any of you gentlemen know where Mr. Valentine headed when he left town?

The men looked at each other blankly. Then the handsome man who had appointed himself spokesman shook his head and said, "Sorry, ma'am. I guess we've let you down.

You might check with the owner of the livery stable, or maybe with the marshal. None of us actually saw the shooting, and it seems none of us saw Valentine leave, either."

"Well, I thank you gentlemen for the information. You have indeed helped me." Suzanne turned away quickly and walked back to the stagecoach. The redhead told the driver to go on without her, for she would catch the next stage. Leaving her luggage at the station, she walked to the marshal's office.

Newton's marshal, Darrell Conway, was sitting at his desk talking to a dapper, stately man when Suzanne Lane walked in. Both men's eyes lit up at the sight of the beautiful woman, and they scrambled to their feet. Conway presumed she had come looking for him, and he said with a smile, "Good evening, ma'am. What can I do for you?"

Suzanne noted the shiny badge on his chest. "Good afternoon, Marshal," she said, returning the smile. "My name is Suzanne Stanwood, and I'm a reporter with the Kansas City *Sun*. I understand you had trouble in your town two days ago from a gunfighter named Johnny Valentine."

"No real trouble, ma'am," he replied.

Her eyes widened. "No real trouble? Valentine killed a man, didn't he? You don't call that trouble?"

The marshal shook his head. "Ma'am, I'm going on fifty years old, and I've been town marshal here from the time the Civil War was over. Ever since then, the West has been crawling with men eager to become famous gunfighters—they don't call this the Wild West for nothing. Gunfights happen often here in Kansas. Crowds gather to watch every one of them, but five minutes after the loser is carried away, the people forget all about it. So as long as the gunfights are fair, I don't call them trouble."

"But from what I understand, Johnny Valentine didn't

even wait around to see if the man he shot down lived or died!" Suzanne exploded. "The man is a murderer, Marshal! A cold-blooded murderer!" The widow's hatred for Valentine was surfacing. "You should have hunted him down. Why didn't you?"

Conway gave his other visitor a sideways glance. Then he looked back at Suzanne and said to her, "Ma'am, I thought you reporters are supposed to report the truth. Well, the truth is, Johnny Valentine's no murderer. I know his reputation, and to my knowledge he has never stepped outside the law. He is a gunfighter, yes—but the only men he kills are those who challenge *him*."

Suzanne thought of how Valentine had gone looking for Frank and had forced him into a shoot-out. She wanted to tell the marshal but thought better of revealing her true purpose for trailing the gunfighter. Cooling herself down, she said more calmly, "So this Charlie Lund challenged Valentine?"

"That's what they tell me, ma'am."

Looking surprised, she asked, "You mean you didn't see the gunfight?"

"No. I was out of town, and I just got back this morning. But I've talked to several of those who witnessed it, and they all tell the same story: Lund pushed Valentine into the gunfight."

The stately man cleared his throat. "Excuse me, Mrs. Stanwood—it is *Mrs*. Stanwood, I presume . . . ?"

"Y-yes, it is, although I'm a widow."

"Oh, forgive me. I didn't mean to intrude into your privacy. . . . My name is Vernon Brewer—I run the bank here in Newton—and it just so happens that I *did* witness the shoot-out. May I confirm that it happened exactly as the marshal has said: Johnny Valentine was indeed challenged by Lund, and although he tried to dissuade Lund, the fellow was bound and determined to try to best Valentine."

"Mr. Brewer, I wonder if you can tell me anything else about Johnny Valentine," Suzanne inquired politely. "For example, do you know where he was heading? You see, I want to do a story about him, but in order to do that I must find him." Suzanne smiled wryly. "I promise you that I do try to be fair and objective in my reporting, gentlemen, and what better way to be able to do so than to meet the man personally."

"I must say, it seems that an awful lot of people are hoping to find the notorious Mr. Valentine of late," Brewer declared.

"Oh?" Suzanne responded, raising her eyebrows.

The marshal looked equally curious. "Have you ever heard of the Jack Decker gang?"

"Yes, I have," she replied.

"They came thundering in here a few hours after Valentine had gone, asking about him. They were told he had left town heading south for Oklahoma, and they stopped just long enough to change horses before they took off after him."

Suzanne Lane was immediately concerned. "Mr. Brewer," she said, "do you think Jack Decker and his gang are friends or foes of Johnny Valentine?"

"Well, I certainly wouldn't know, but from the looks on their faces as they rode by me, my guess is they are Mr. Valentine's foes."

Suzanne held her face taut, masking the feelings that were churning inside her at that moment. If the Decker gang was chasing Valentine to kill him, they had a head start on her. *No!* she thought. *They can't take that pleasure away from me. I want the right to kill him myself!* Forcing this unwelcome wrinkle from her mind, the determined widow told herself that possibly Decker was not following Valentine to kill him—or that even if he was, somehow the just hands of fate would let her get to Johnny Valentine before Decker did.

The marshal's voice brought Suzanne back from her thoughts.

"Vernon," he grunted angrily, "why wasn't I told that the Decker gang had been here? You know I should be advised of something like that."

Brewer shrugged his shoulders. "I'm sorry, Darrell. I didn't think it mattered since they left town right away in search of Valentine."

"Any time that bloody bunch is around, I want to know it," Conway said sternly.

Suzanne interrupted the exchange. "Well, gentlemen, thank you very much for all your help. I must be going now."

She opened the door and was about to make her exit when a rider came skidding to a halt in front of the office, shouting the marshal's name.

Leaping from his lathered mount, the man almost plowed into Suzanne in his hurry to go through the door. "Marshal!" the man gasped. "I just rode up from Wichita. The sheriff there got a wire late this morning from the town marshal down in Iuka. A band of Kiowas massacred six white men, travelers, near there early this morning. The Indians scalped every one of 'em and mutilated their bodies!"

Suzanne Lane was shocked to learn that there were once again hostile Kiowas in Kansas. The Army had herded Chief Kicking Bird and his tribe onto a reservation in Oklahoma nearly four years previously.

"I came as fast as I could, Marshal. I figured you'd want to know so's people around here could be warned and be on the lookout for 'em."

"You bet." Conway nodded. "Any idea how many are in the war party?"

"About forty, Marshal," the man replied. "Apparently they're out to spill all the blood they can. The information I got in Wichita is that a few weeks ago the Indian agents visited the reservation there in Oklahoma, and Chief Kicking Bird told them some bad news. A renegade Kiowa subchief named Trailing-the-Enemy worked up a bunch of warriors into a frenzy to kill white men. Then they all jumped the reservation and went on the warpath. Kicking Bird doesn't want any trouble with the whites, but Trailing-the-Enemy wants revenge for what the whites have done to his people over the years, and he's decided to take out his vengeance on whites at random. So far the renegades have successfully eluded the Army."

The marshal clapped the rider on the shoulder. "Thanks for telling me, Hank. I'd better go spread the word. Vernon, get the town council together and tell them about this. We'd better be prepared. Tell everybody you meet to keep a sharp eye. And nobody should go anywhere without guns."

Suzanne Lane was about to leave the office when the marshal said to her, "Mrs. Stanwood, maybe you ought to reconsider doing your story at this time. It might be a lot safer if you were to head straight back to Kansas City and forget about looking for Johnny Valentine in this part of Kansas."

"Well, I'll be," the man named Hank declared. "Funny you should mention Valentine's name."

Suzanne's head swiveled around, and she looked at the man, waiting for him to continue.

"The sheriff in Iuka was tellin' me that Valentine was challenged there yesterday by a greenhorn kid," Hank went on. "But Valentine talked the kid out of it and let him live."

"Guess there's a streak of mercy in him," mused the marshal.

*Then why didn't he show some of it to Frank?* Suzanne thought bitterly. Aloud, she said to Hank, "Well, I guess you've arrived in the nick of time, sir. Now I know in which direction to head."

Conway shook his head and was about to speak, but Suzanne continued before he could protest. "I won't be dissuaded from my pursuit, Marshal. From the sound of it, by the time I catch up with Johnny Valentine, I may have a story long enough to fill an entire weekly issue of my newspaper. Thank you again, gentlemen."

Suzanne left the office and headed back for the stage depot. She wondered if the Decker gang had also learned which way Valentine was headed. She hoped not.

She had to admit that she was fearful of continuing with a band of renegade Kiowas on the warpath, but the desire burning within her to track down and kill Johnny Valentine overrode her fear.

Her footsteps resounded on the boardwalk as she quickened her pace toward the stage-line office.

# Chapter Five

Early the next morning Suzanne Lane boarded the stagecoach and headed west toward Iuka. The stage, bound ultimately for Dodge City, would make several stops along the way; the five passengers, the driver, and the shotgunner were scheduled to spend the night in Iuka, the very town where Johnny Valentine had last been seen.

Following a hunch, Suzanne reasoned that Valentine would probably continue on to Dodge. It was about the last place a rider could stop for supplies before heading in any direction across the empty stretches of west Kansas.

As the coach rocked along, the passengers introduced themselves. Suzanne, seated next to a window, had two elderly spinsters to her left. One, Edith Gardner, was eighty-one. The other was Edith's companion, seventy-seven-year-old Sadie Ketcham. Across from the three ladies sat Barney Zylstra, a retired merchant, and his wife, Mattie. The spinsters were bound for Fellsburg, and the Zylstras were going to Dodge City.

For some time the main topic of conversation between the passengers was the Indian threat, but then the discussion slowly died out, and each person lapsed into private thought.

While her husband snored softly beside her, Mattie Zylstra surreptitiously admired the lovely redheaded woman through eyes that were surrounded by a net of time-induced wrinkles. She had the urge to tell Suzanne to enjoy her youthful beauty while she had it; age would soon steal it from her. But she thought better of it, knowing it was not her place to do so.

Suzanne Lane was feeling mixed emotions—those of missing Frank and hating Johnny Valentine. Her husband's killer would stop traveling sooner or later, and when he did, Suzanne would find him and carry out the execution. Exacting vengeance on Johnny Valentine was her only goal in life right now, and she would not rest until the man had died by her hand. Squeezing her purse with her fingers, she felt the reassuring bulge of Frank's .38 revolver. Valentine's days were numbered.

When the passengers were deposited in front of the Iuka Hotel that evening, Suzanne was eager to check in and put her bag in her room, then come back downstairs and talk with some of the townspeople. Knowing that Johnny Valentine had been in Iuka, she reasoned that it was likely someone could tell her whether he did in fact continue west toward Dodge.

She did not have far to go before finding her answer. Approaching a man in the hotel lobby, she found out that her hunch was right: Valentine had indeed ridden west right after he had backed down the young greenhorn gunfighter.

Walking around the small town to see if she could learn anything more, Suzanne found that Johnny Valentine's presence paled in importance beside the recent massacre by the renegade Kiowas. There was fear that the Indians would kill again; Trailing-the-Enemy had a reputation of being bloodthirsty and fierce.

The talk of more massacres instilled caution in the crew and passengers of the stagecoach. When it was time to pull out early the next morning, Barney Zylstra took the driver aside so he could not be overheard and asked him, "Do you gentlemen think it's safe to travel on? I certainly wouldn't want to put my wife in any danger—nor any of the other ladies, for that matter."

J. M. Sego replied, "I can't guarantee you that it's safe, Mr. Zylstra; however, I can tell you that I plan on celebrating my sixty-third birthday next spring. That is to say, I've driven a stagecoach for many, many years, and I don't believe in taking foolish chances. My feeling is that as long as there's only one band of Kiowas on the loose, our chances of running into them are remote. But if you and your wife don't care to continue, why, that's your privilege. But the Butterfield Overland Mail Company has got to keep moving."

The young shotgunner, Rick Linn, suggested, "J.M., maybe we'd better ask the ladies themselves if they want to go on. They might want to stay here in Iuka until Trailing-the-Enemy and his bunch have been run down by the army."

Sego nodded. The three men returned to where the ladies were waiting beside the coach, and Sego explained that the odds were with them that they would not see the Kiowas, but that it was still quite possible.

There was a short discussion. The spinsters decided that since Fellsburg was only twenty-five miles from Iuka, they would take the chance. The Zylstras agreed with each other that they would gamble it. Suzanne Lane dreaded the thought of meeting up with the Indians, but her need for vengeance was too strong to allow her to pause in her pursuit of the man who had gunned down her husband. She decided to go on with the rest of them.

The young shotgunner gave his hand to each of the spinsters and helped them into the coach. Suzanne politely told the Zylstras to board next. While they were climbing in, Rick Linn stood next to Suzanne, waiting to help her in. He turned to her, and his boyish face blushed slightly. "Miz Stanwood, ma'am, I, uh . . . I hope you won't take me as being brash, but I just have to tell you that I think you are the prettiest woman I've seen in all my twenty-one years."

It was the redhead's turn to blush. Smiling warmly, she reached out and patted his cheek. "Thank you, Rick," she said, tilting her head slightly. "That's the nicest compliment I have ever had."

Struck by her beauty and unable to say more, Linn gave her his hand and helped her into the coach. Suzanne settled in the seat and smiled at him once again. Then he closed the door and climbed up into the box.

As the stage rolled out of Iuka, Suzanne felt the bulk of the .38 revolver in her purse and wondered how the young shotgunner would feel about her if he knew the real reason for her mission.

When the stage passed the town cemetery, Suzanne smiled to herself. With luck, Johnny Valentine would soon find reason to settle in one place long enough for her to catch up to him—and wherever that was, the local cemetery would have one new grave.

The pitching and rolling of the stagecoach lulled the passengers into a stupor. But forty minutes after leaving Iuka, everyone sat up as the coach slowed where the road dipped down into a ravine. On the far side of the ravine, the stage had to squeeze between two huge boulders as it pulled onto the crest.

As the stage moved cautiously between the boulders, a lone gunman wearing a bandanna over the lower part of his face suddenly stood up on the boulder to the right. Brandishing a cocked revolver, his eyes wild, he barked through the bandanna, "Hold it right there or you die!"

The man clearly had the drop on them.

J. M. Sego pulled back on the reins, and Barney Zylstra's face appeared in the window.

The robber bellowed, "Pull somethin' funny, mister, and I'll be happy to blow your head off! Now move ahead real slow and stop the stage just past the boulders."

When the stage was where he wanted it, the outlaw hopped quickly to the ground, waving the gun threateningly and commanding the passengers to get out of the coach with their hands in the air. Looking up at the driver and shotgunner in the box, he snapped, "You two! Throw your guns on the ground, then climb down one at a time. And don't even think of tryin' anything stupid!"

After two revolvers, a rifle, and Linn's shotgun had dropped to the dust, J. M. Sego climbed down from the stage, with Rick Linn following. The robber lined everyone up alongside the coach, and then he pulled a cloth sack from under his belt.

Starting with Sego, who was first in line, the robber aimed the muzzle of his gun at the driver's chest. Extending the sack toward him with the other hand, he said, "Empty your pockets into the sack, mister. I want that gold watch in your vest, too."

Reluctantly, Sego obeyed, glaring at the man the whole time. Linn was next, and he stared at the robber woodenly while the man relieved him of his wallet, watch, and loose change. The robber met his gaze over the bandanna and said, "If you're thinkin' of tryin' what I read in your eyes, kid, forget it. You'll die on your feet."

Cold chills danced along Suzanne Lane's spine as the

robber moved down the line to Barney Zylstra. She was thinking that when she emptied her purse into the sack, her gun would have to go with it. An angry knot settled in her stomach; she wanted to use Frank's gun to kill Johnny Valentine. The anger spread throughout her body. If she could only get her gun out before the robber reached her . . .

Suzanne wondered if she dared lower her hands and reach inside her drawstring purse, which was dangling from her arm. Then she realized that such a move would be foolish: the robber's eyes were darting about, watching everyone closely.

Suddenly, as the robber shifted toward Mattie Zylstra, Rick Linn went into action. When the muzzle of the robber's gun was between Barney and Mattie, Linn lunged for the robber's gun hand. The revolver roared, sending the slug into the coach, and although no one was hurt, Sadie Ketcham began screaming at the top of her lungs.

Linn wrestled briefly with the robber, but the man was too strong. He twisted the weapon against the shotgunner's body, snapped back the hammer, and fired. Rick Linn went down with the bullet in his side, and Sadie's screams grew even louder.

The robber saw J. M. Sego heading for him and swung the gun in time to connect with the older man's jaw. Sego slumped to his knees, shaking his head.

The robber thumbed back the hammer and was about to shoot Sego, but Sadie Ketcham's incessant screaming was a source of infuriating irritation. The woman stood with fists clenched, eyes bulging, body rigid, and mouth open wide. Her screams were ear-piercing.

The masked man stomped over to Sadie and hollered above her wailing, "Shut up, old woman! Shut up, or I'll kill you!"

The added terror served only to increase Sadie's volume, though. Swearing, the robber put the gun between her eyes and pulled the trigger. As the gun bucked in his hand a black hole appeared in the spinster's forehead. Blood sprayed the stagecoach as Sadie slammed against it, then slumped to the ground.

The Zylstras and Edith Gardner gasped loudly and hastily stepped away, clinging to each other, eyes wide with fear. J. M. Sego was still on his knees, trying to clear his brain, while Rick Linn lay on the ground, helplessly eyeing the shotgun that lay out of his reach.

Linn clutched his bleeding side and swore at the bandit in fury, yelling, "You filthy animal! She was an old woman!"

Shocked beyond measure by the brutal events that had transpired so quickly, Suzanne was momentarily dazed. Then she realized that no one was paying attention to her and she could take the gun from her purse without detection. Her hands were already moving down toward it as the vile killer turned to confront Linn. Her right hand dipped into the purse, and as the masked man snapped back the hammer of his weapon and was bringing it to bear on the wounded shotgunner, Suzanne's gun roared.

The .38 slug tore into the man's back. He buckled, grunting from the impact, then staggered around, still holding his gun. His eyes were like burning coals above the bandanna. He was attempting to aim his gun at her as his weakening legs struggled to hold him. Suzanne saw he had enough life left in him to kill.

Coolly the redhead cocked her gun, aimed at his face, and fired again. The bullet chewed into the bridge of his nose and snapped his head back violently. He flopped backward, falling over Rick Linn.

The shotgunner squirmed, kicked the corpse off him, and tried to get up.

Suzanne dashed to him, saying, "You'd better stay still, Mr. Linn, until I can get the bleeding stopped." She dropped her revolver back into her purse, then bent down and tended to the young man.

Mattie Zylstra went over to Edith Gardner, who was sobbing uncontrollably, and put her arm around her. She helped the elderly woman into the coach, saying, "There, there, Miss Gardner. It's all over now."

Looking out through the open door at Sadie's body lying crumpled on the ground, Edith whimpered.

Sego, still feeling the effects of the blow of the gun barrel, was helped to his feet by Zylstra. They stood over Suzanne, watching while she used a torn piece of her petticoat to bind Rick Linn's wound and stop the flow of blood.

Zylstra remarked, "Mrs. Stanwood, I'm amazed at how professionally you handled your gun. If I didn't know better, I'd think you were an experienced soldier or lawman."

The realization that she had just shot a man, killing him, started to sink in. Suzanne swayed slightly as she touched her temples and said, "I guess I just reacted instinctively. I . . . I've never killed anyone before, I assure you."

"Well, you certainly took control of things mighty handily," Sego said.

"It . . . it had to be done, so I did it," she said. She sighed and then turned back to tending the wounded shotgunner.

Wrapping Sadie Ketcham's body in the tarpaulin that covered the luggage, Sego and Zylstra struggled together to lay the body on top of the coach.

Suzanne helped Rick Linn climb in, then sat beside him. She knew the bullet had to be taken out very soon. Though the tide of blood had been slowed by the make-shift bandage, he was still losing it steadily. He had to have a doctor's care as soon as possible.

Picking up the guns and the cloth sack, Sego and Zylstra

climbed on top of the stage, and seconds later the stage-coach was racing toward Fellsburg. The robber's lifeless body was left for disposal by carnivorous birds and animals.

As the westbound stagecoach bearing Suzanne Lane made its way toward Fellsburg, Kansas, the Decker gang was racing to Dodge City. Johnny Valentine's ruse of heading south from Wichita had not fooled Jack Decker for long, and with vengeance burning in his veins, the outlaw led his men to Dodge, hoping they would find the gunfighter there.

It was just after three o'clock in the afternoon when the gang galloped into Dodge City on gasping, lathered horses. Hauling up in front of the most popular of the town's many saloons, they tied their heaving mounts to the hitch rails and stepped onto the boardwalk. In every town they had come to in their search for Valentine, they had checked out the barrooms first, since word of a stranger in town seemed to hit the drinking establishments right away— even if the stranger never swung a batwing door. Decker and his men also knew that a man who rides hard gets thirsty, and a saloon is the first place he will stop.

Standing in front of the Long Branch Saloon, Decker paused a moment, almost sniffing the air. He looked at his men gathered around him and growled, "Valentine's here—or he's right nearby. I can feel it." Pointing to the black patch that covered the left eye he had lost in a saloon brawl years before, the outlaw leader declared, "This thing always starts throbbing when I'm near my prey. It ain't led me wrong yet—and it's throbbing right now."

His right-hand man, Nick Hotchkiss, grunted, "I'll go in myself and take a look around. If I see Valentine, I'll come back out and point him out to you." Short, stocky, and very muscular, Hotchkiss was younger than Decker by five years and even more cold-blooded than his boss. Even the other gang members thought he had ice instead of blood in his veins, figuring there was no other reason for Hotchkiss's hatred for humanity, his love for killing, and his total lack of mercy.

Decker chuckled. "It's lucky you saw him in that shoot-out down in Abilene three years ago. Otherwise we might not know who our target is. Okay, go on in—but make it quick."

Hotchkiss sauntered through the batwing doors of the saloon, one of Dodge City's biggest and fanciest, and the favorite establishment of Bat Masterson and his brothers a few years back. Decker and his gang members were thankful that those famous lawmen were no longer present to make trouble for them.

Decker stood in front of the saloon, pacing impatiently, and when Hotchkiss pushed his way out through the swinging doors ten minutes later, shaking his head negatively, Decker suddenly lashed out at him. "What took you so long?" the gang leader exploded. "Did you stop to admire all them pictures linin' the walls? This ain't no pleasure jaunt, Nick!" the gang leader exploded.

"If you don't like the way I'm doing things, go on and find Valentine yourself—if you can," Hotchkiss angrily retorted. "This place ain't no little barroom in some backwater town, Jack. There's gotta be dozens of people in there."

"Yeah, okay, okay," Decker mumbled. "Let's try the next one."

Decker and his men spent the next hour and a half walking first down one side of the street and then the other, poking their heads into every saloon they came to. Coming out of the Lady Gay saloon, Hotchkiss suddenly stopped. Turning to Decker, he said, "Jack, it don't look like Valentine's here after all. Maybe we was wrong. Maybe he *did* head back to Texas. Maybe—"

"I ain't wrong!" Decker growled. Reaching up and touching his eye patch again, he declared, "We're getting closer. I just know it."

His men looked at each other doubtfully, but they obediently followed their leader along the boardwalk until they were standing in front of the Silver Saddle Saloon. Turning to Nick Hotchkiss, Decker said, "Okay, Nick, you—"

Jack Decker's attention was suddenly arrested by a tall, lean man with a U.S. marshal's badge pinned on his chest. He was coming out of the tobacco shop next to the saloon.

The handsome, clean-shaven lawman was biting the tip off a cigar when he spotted Decker. He ambled up to the outlaw leader, coolly appraised him, and asked, "What are you doing in these parts, Jack?"

Decker casually adjusted the patch over his eye. "Just ridin' through, Marshal," he replied levelly.

Running a discerning gaze over the motley group, the marshal said, "Why don't you introduce me to your gang members, Jack?"

"Gang members?" echoed Decker. "They ain't no gang members, Marshal. They're my business associates." Clearing his throat, he flicked a glance at his men and said cloyingly, "Fellas, I want you to meet United States Marshal Ford Gunnison. Back when I hadn't learned the error of my ways and was still livin' outside the law, Marshal Gunnison arrested me and took me to trial. I did five years for my crimes."

Looking the gang over again, Gunnison pushed his hat back and scratched his tawny hair. "I've been back East so I haven't heard anything about you for a while, but something tells me you're still in the outlaw business, Jack."

Decker took the weight off his game leg and guffawed. "Aw, Marshal, you've got a great sense of humor. But no, sir, I swear I'm clean. I did my time and I'm walkin' inside the law."

Gunnison pulled a match from a shirt pocket, struck it on the heel of his boot, and lighted his cigar. Looking down at the small man through a cloud of smoke, he said sternly, "You'd better stay clean, Decker, if you know what's good for you. Next time I send you up, you won't get off so easy." The lawman gave the outlaw a wary look and then pushed his way through the batwings of the Silver Saddle Saloon.

Decker peered over the top of the swinging doors until he was satisfied that Gunnison's attention was elsewhere. Then he turned to his top man. "Okay, Nick, go in and see if you can spot Valentine."

Again Decker waited outside, impatiently pacing back and forth.

Finally Hotchkiss reappeared with a smirk on his face and nodded. "He's in there, all right. He's standing at the far end of the bar, drinkin' a beer."

"Are you sure it was Valentine?"

"Sure enough. I couldn't see him full face, and it's awful smoky in there, but I could plainly see his profile and the color of his hair and his tall, thin frame. It's him, all right."

A wicked sneer curled Decker's mouth. He turned to the others and said, "Okay, boys, this is it. I've changed my mind about wantin' him to die slow. We'll get ourselves positioned so we can catch Valentine in a cross fire when he comes out that door. Don't be obvious about what you're doin'. We don't want to draw attention to ourselves. Just be ready. I want him so full of holes, even his own mother wouldn't recognize him."

"What if the marshal sticks his nose in?" asked Hotchkiss.

"Shoot it off for him," Decker grunted bitterly.

Each member of the gang tried to make himself appear to be casually standing at rest, but their eyes were pinned on the batwings of the Silver Saddle.

A half hour passed before Valentine came through the door, placing his broad-brimmed hat on his sand-colored head. Nick Hotchkiss waited next to his boss. "That's him!" he whispered.

From his place beside his horse, Decker shouted sharply, "Hey, Valentine!"

The tall man looked to see who had called him.

"This is for Danny Wellman!"

The street suddenly erupted with gunfire as bullets tore into Valentine, hitting him and a man standing right behind him. Over twenty-five lead slugs ripped into Valentine's body as he was repeatedly jerked around. When the firing stopped, the body sagged to the ground, and blood flowed in every direction.

There were shouts and screams along the street as the Decker bunch mounted up fast and galloped out of Dodge City.

# Chapter Six

Suzanne Lane's stagecoach reached Dodge City the day after the shooting at the Silver Saddle Saloon. After arriving in town, Suzanne was in the restaurant of the Plains Hotel, having dinner, when she overheard two other diners discussing how Johnny Valentine had heard gunned down.

The color drained from her face, and she dropped her fork. Turning toward a distinguished-looking man, she said weakly, "Excuse me, I didn't mean to eavesdrop, but did I hear you correctly? Did you say Johnny Valentine, the gunfighter, was killed here yesterday?"

The man plucked at the end of his silver mustache. "Why, yes, ma'am. He was ambushed by the Jack Decker gang as he walked out of the saloon. He was buried in Boot Hill within hours."

"I see," Suzanne said. "Thank you." No longer hungry, the widow pushed aside her plate. She stared blankly at it for several moments before getting up and walking to the cashier's desk.

In a daze Suzanne walked to her hotel and climbed the stairs to her room. Entering it, she slammed the door hard, her anger and frustration taking control of her. She threw her purse on the bed and started pacing the floor. Wringing her hands and cursing Jack Decker, she condemned him to the blazing regions below. Now she would never learn what Frank's connection to Johnny Valentine had been—and worse yet, she had been cheated out of killing Valentine personally.

Tears clouded Suzanne's eyes as she continued pacing. Speaking aloud in a hoarse whisper, she said angrily, "It isn't right. It just isn't right. Frank was my husband. *I* had the right to kill Valentine!" Completely defeated, she threw herself on the bed, weeping and swearing until her strength was spent.

After a sleepless night Suzanne Lane left her room at dawn and walked the half mile to Boot Hill. Threading her way among the gravestones, she found what she was looking for. At the head of a fresh grave stood a simple wooden marker that read:

*Johnny Valentine*
*Shot to Death*
*July 9, 1882*

Frustration washed through Suzanne again as tears came to her eyes and her lips quivered. Looking down at the mound of newly turned dirt, she sobbed, "Why did you do it, Johnny Valentine? Why did you kill Frank? What awful thing had he done that made you feel he deserved to die?"

Suzanne stood beside the grave until she had regained control of her emotions. Then, leaving Boot Hill, she walked back into Dodge City and went to the Butterfield Overland office. Her journey over, there was no need to continue her masquerade. Using her married name, she bought passage on the stage leaving at ten-thirty that morning for Great Bend. All she could do now was go home and try to put her life back together.

The redheaded woman left the hotel at ten-fifteen, carrying her purse and suitcase. She had walked about halfway to the stage office when a tall, lean man came up beside her.

The man touched the brim of his pale gray Stetson as he smiled and said, "Are you going to the stage office, ma'am?"

Suzanne Lane had had more than her share of masculine attention, and it was not unusual for a man to offer his assistance, just to be near her for a few minutes. She focused on the gold-plated badge that adorned the man's vest, then looked up at his handsome face. Without breaking stride, she said, "Yes, I am."

"May I have the pleasure of carrying your traveling bag for you?"

Finally stopping, she smiled at the lawman and said, "Why, yes. You may."

The lovely widow felt instantly at ease with the man who wore the U.S. marshal's badge. He was very well turned out, from his neatly trimmed hair to his three-piece, charcoal-gray, pin-striped suit. Only the well-worn holster peeking out from his coat detracted from his otherwise impeccable appearance.

As he took Suzanne Lane's suitcase from her, he told her, "My name is Ford Gunnison, ma'am. United States Marshal Ford Gunnison."

"And I'm Suzanne Lane," she responded, extending her hand with a smile.

The rangy lawman shook her hand delicately, asking, "Are you taking the ten-thirty stage?"

"Yes, I am. I live in Great Bend."

"Well, we'll be fellow passengers. I'm taking the same stage, only I'll be staying on and going farther north."

"It will be good having a lawman aboard," Suzanne said as they reached the stage office. "You know . . . with all the highwaymen around."

"Thank you, ma'am."

"And the hostile Kiowas, too."

"Yes, ma'am," the handsome marshal agreed as he eyed her beauty surreptitiously.

Four other people were waiting to board the stagecoach with Suzanne Lane and the federal man. They were Oliver and Pearl Madison, a well-dressed couple in their late thirties, an elderly physician named Dr. Burke Simms, and a mean-eyed man wearing a low-slung holster who introduced himself as Sid Bingham. The other passengers recoiled slightly, for Bingham was a well-known gunfighter, and upon hearing his name, Suzanne was even more pleased that a marshal was along on the journey.

The Madisons, who were also from Great Bend, were acquainted with Suzanne Lane. They exchanged greetings, saying how lucky they were to have such pleasant weather for their trip.

"And thank goodness those Kiowas who've been causing trouble are well to the south. I guess all we have to worry about is some stray bandit—and with the marshal riding with us, we shouldn't have too much trouble defending ourselves," declared Oliver Madison.

Suzanne smiled. "That's exactly what I told Mr. Gunnison."

The glances between the gunfighter and the marshal were far more strained than those between the other passengers, but since Bingham was not a wanted man, both men soon relaxed.

When the passengers started boarding the coach, Suzanne climbed in first, with Pearl and Oliver Madison following and sitting alongside her. Ford Gunnison climbed in and took the seat opposite Suzanne. He was followed by Sid Bingham and Burke Simms.

The stage was hardly out of Dodge City when Suzanne felt the gunfighter's eyes on her. When she met his gaze, he grinned lecherously, tugging at his bushy mustache. Glaring at him momentarily, she turned toward the woman on her left.

"What brought you and Oliver to Dodge City?" she asked politely, determined to keep her mind from dwelling on her unsuccessful journey.

Pearl Madison, struggling to keep a lock of her brown hair from bouncing into her eyes, smiled and answered, "Oliver's brother and his family are there, and we visited with them for almost a month. It had been quite some time since we'd seen them, so we decided to have a nice long reunion."

Pearl then looked over at the physician and said, "That reminds me, Dr. Simms, when Oliver's family saw you waiting at the stage office, they told me that you've been practicing medicine in Dodge City for more than thirty years."

"Yes, ma'am," Simms said, nodding proudly. "Thirty-five, to be exact. And now my son recently graduated medical school, and he's joined me as my partner. In fact, it's because I was able to leave the practice in his capable hands that I could take this little trip. I'm going to Salina, to visit with friends."

As Suzanne listened to Pearl commenting on how nice it must be for the doctor to have his son working with him, she felt Sid Bingham's eyes on her once again. Her face was like granite as she again glared briefly at the gunfighter.

Bingham looked to his left and let his gaze settle on the marshal. The gunfighter was sure the lawman's good looks and dapper clothes made him a hit with the ladies. He noted that the well-worn holster on Gunnison's right hip carried the short-barrel Colt .45 for a faster draw. No doubt the man was good with the gun.

When the federal man noticed Bingham studying him, he fixed him with a steely glare and asked pointedly, "You got a problem?"

The gunfighter curled his lip and said, "I don't cotton to lawmen. That ain't against the law, is it?"

"Nope," came the marshal's tart reply. "You don't have to cotton to me—just quit studying me."

Bingham shrugged his shoulders and once more let his gaze rest on the fascinating redhead across from him.

The two women were chatting again. Pearl asked, "Were you in Dodge on business, Suzanne? And how is Frank? Is that husband of yours still as busy as ever?"

Suzanne's face pinched, and her eyes instantly brimmed with tears.

Seeing her distress, Pearl said quickly, "Oh, dear, did I say something wrong?"

All eyes were on Suzanne as she answered with quivering lips, "Frank is . . . he's dead."

"Dead!" exclaimed Pearl, her eyes wide. "Oh, my goodness."

Oliver leaned toward her and asked, "I'm so sorry, Suzanne. Was he ill?"

Reaching into her purse for a handkerchief, the widow said bitterly, "No, he was murdered—in Junction City, by the same man who was gunned down in Dodge City the day before yesterday."

"By Johnny Valentine?" gasped Oliver.

"Yes," Suzanne said, nodding.

"How did it happen?"

"Valentine challenged him." She told them of the events as the Butterfield stage employees had related them to her, and then she added, "So Frank knew he had only one chance against a professional gunfighter. He always carried a gun in his coat—just for protection, since he traveled so much on business, carrying large sums of money from the stores." Suzanne's voice broke, and she struggled to compose herself. "When Frank pulled out his gun to defend himself, somebody yelled a warning to Valentine. That killer just spun around and shot my Frank dead. As far as I'm concerned, it was nothing short of murder."

Burke Simms rubbed his jaw and said, "Mrs. Lane, with all the sympathy in the world in your time of grief, may I respectfully say one thing? The Valentine family used to live in Dodge. I delivered all three of the children—Johnny, Emma, and Jim. I know them all quite well. Nice parents and good kids. Last time I saw Johnny, he was about fifteen, a real gentle-natured boy. Reports I've heard through the years say he only kills in self-defense. I can't believe Johnny would force a man into a gunfight like the one you've just described unless he had a mighty good reason."

With her green eyes blazing, the widow snapped bitterly, "Then why was he forcing my husband to draw against him?"

"Can't answer that, ma'am," replied the silver-haired physician. "But the fact he was going to give your husband a chance to draw against him proves Johnny was no murderer. And I'll guarantee you this much: For Johnny to have approached your husband like that, he was plenty mad about something."

Suzanne settled back in her seat and put a shaky hand to her mouth.

"I'm sorry about your husband, ma'am," said the doctor, "but I knew Johnny Valentine. I can't let his memory be stained by labeling him a murderer when I know better. Please, don't judge him until you have obtained all the facts."

Suzanne blinked against her tears and wiped them with

the handkerchief. *But there's no way I can know all the facts now that both men are dead!* she said to herself. *Why Valentine wanted to kill Frank is a secret they took to their graves.*

Dr. Simms reached over and patted Suzanne's hand. "I'm sorry. I hope I didn't upset you too much," he said tenderly.

Forcing a slight smile, she said, "I'll be all right. Thank you."

Oliver Madison swerved the conversation in another direction. Looking over at the lawman, he cleared his throat and asked, "Where are you traveling to, Marshal Gunnison?"

"I'm heading for Topeka to report in at the chief U.S. marshal's office there." He paused and shook his head, saying with a slight smile, "I almost didn't make this trip. I stopped in Dodge the day before yesterday and nearly got myself killed when the Decker gang ambushed Johnny Valentine. I was coming out of the saloon just behind him when somebody shouted Valentine's name and the bullets started flying. I had to drop flat on the floor to keep from being hit. Then suddenly it was all over, and the gang was gone before I could do anything about it. Soon as I make my report in Topeka, I'm going after Decker and his men."

Sid Bingham snorted. "That's too bad."

"What is, Bingham?" Gunnison asked wryly. "That I wasn't killed?"

"Now, Marshal, you're putting words in my mouth." He pulled out a cigar, biting off the end of it and spitting it out the window. "Anybody mind if I smoke?"

"Yes, I do," said Pearl Madison.

Bingham shrugged his shoulders and struck a match against his boot.

"My wife said she minds if you smoke, Bingham!" Oliver Madison said heatedly.

When the gunfighter ignored the protest and, grinning insolently, lit the cigar, the marshal grabbed it and threw it out the window. Bingham swore and swung his right fist at the lawman's jaw, but the marshal blocked the punch and sent one of his own, and fist met jawbone. Bingham was stunned. The coach lurched as the other passengers scrambled to get out of the way of the flailing elbows.

"What's goin' on down there?" Floyd Bates yelled from up top.

"Driver, stop the stage!" the lawman shouted out the window.

When the vehicle rolled to a halt, the marshal opened the door and shoved Bingham out with his foot. The gunfighter hit the ground, rolling in the dirt, his hat sailing off his head.

The lawman stepped out and stood over the gunfighter. "How would you like to walk the rest of the way, Bingham?"

Rolling to his knees, the gunfighter shook his head and tried to clear his vision. He staggered to his feet, glaring at the lawman, and then picked up his hat. Flicking it against his thigh to get rid of the dust, he said defiantly, "You ain't got no right to put me off the stage, Gunnison."

"If he don't, I do! As captain of this ship, I say who rides and who don't."

Both men on the ground looked up at Floyd Bates in the driver's box.

Bates eyed his shotgunner and asked, "Well, Sam, what do you think?"

"Mr. Bates, I'm a mere twenty-three while you're all of fifty, so I'll defer to the superior wisdom that comes with age," Sam Todd said with amusement.

"Smart lad!" Bates declared with a grin. He looked down at the gunfighter and glared at him. Then shifting his gaze to the tall lawman, he asked, "What's your opinion, Marshal?"

"If he behaves, I say we give him another chance," Gunnison answered. "If not—"

"I ain't gonna cause no more trouble," Bingham cut in.

Suzanne Lane decided that now was the time to speak her mind. Stepping down from the coach, she drew close to the lawman and looked coldly at Bingham. "Before you let him back on the stage, Marshal Gunnison," she said, "I want him to promise that he'll stop looking at me with his filthy eyes."

"What do you mean?" asked the federal man.

"He keeps leering at me. Tell him to keep his eyes to himself."

The marshal's eyes bored into the gunfighter as he said icily, "One more look, Bingham, and not only will I throw you off the stage, I'll break every bone in your body. Got it?"

Sid Bingham nodded. "Yeah."

"Then get back on board and practice being a model citizen."

The gunfighter boarded the coach, and Suzanne looked up at the lawman. For a brief moment their eyes locked, and something strange and unexplainable passed silently between them. The sensation sent a tingle through Suzanne's body, and although it was pleasurable, it frightened her, and she looked away.

"Thank you, Marshal," she said, looking down at her feet. "I'm very grateful for your help. I don't think Bingham will bother me anymore."

After the lawman and the widow had reboarded the stage, the journey started again. The rocking vehicle rolled steadily across the flat Kansas prairie. By midafternoon they pulled into a relay station on the edge of a village

called Kinsley and enjoyed a welcome stop and a good
meal.

Ominous dark thunderheads were gathering on the western horizon as the stage continued northeast toward Great
Bend. Up in the box, Floyd Bates and Sam Todd hunched
down to protect themselves from the rising wind.

Inside the coach, Suzanne was looking out the window
toward the west, peering at the swirling black clouds that
were covering more of the sky every minute. Then she felt
Sid Bingham's gaze on her again, and her eyes narrowed
with annoyance. Looking first at the gunfighter, she then
glanced meaningfully at the marshal, then back to Bingham.
The gunfighter got the message quickly and turned to look
out the window.

Suzanne smiled with satisfaction and glanced again at
the marshal, whose distant expression made her recall that
magic moment when the stage was stopped. A flame had
ignited between her and Ford Gunnison. Neither had
commented on it, but it was there. She had read it in his
eyes, and she knew he had read it in hers. Suzanne was
struck with guilt. She should not be feeling this way
toward another man so soon after Frank's death. . . .

. . . Or should she? What did she and Frank really have
left between them these past several months? Nothing.
Until now she had never admitted to herself that her love
for Frank had faded, but the cold, hard fact was that it
had. The sensation that she had felt when looking at the
handsome marsh ' had brought that realization to the
surface.

Suzanne looked steadily across at Ford Gunnison until
he felt her gaze. Their eyes locked again, and the same
feeling surged through her once more. The handsome
man smiled at her warmly, looking deep into her eyes,
and Suzanne's heart leaped in her breast.

Suddenly a disturbing thought came to her. What if she was mistaken about what she read in his eyes? What if he was married? Biting her lower lip, she looked out the window again, oblivious to the dark clouds swirling closer. She swung her gaze back to the marshal. He had not taken his eyes off her. He smiled again.

*Relax, Suzanne*, she told herself. *That look in his eyes and the smile he is giving you suggest that neither are you mistaken nor is he married.*

The stage was about five miles beyond the town of Larned when Sam Todd elbowed the driver and pointed to a man running through a field to the right of the road, frantically waving his arms. Bates slowed the team, preparing to stop.

The passengers looked out to see why they were slowing down, and when they spotted the man, Oliver Madison said, "I hope this isn't some kind of trick in order to try and rob us," but they realized that the anguish on the man's face was real.

As the stage squeaked to a stop, the man leaned against it, white-faced and gasping for breath, and looked up at the crewmen. "Please! You gotta help me!" he said to the two men in the box. "My name's Gene McKee. Three Kiowa Indians attacked me and my partner." Pointing to the tall grass behind him, he gasped, "My partner is out there, wounded bad. Please, help me!"

Both driver and shotgunner climbed down from the box. At the same moment the coach doors came open, and the passengers began filing out.

"I'm a doctor, Mr. McKee," Burke Simms declared, black bag in hand. "Take me to your friend."

"Oh, thank God!" the man exclaimed. "Follow me, Doc!" He headed toward the spot where his friend lay.

The marshal followed Simms and Gene McKee, and

when they reached the injured man, who was passed out in the grass about a hundred yards from the road, Dr. Simms examined the bullet wound in the man's abdomen. "The slug is still in there. I'll have to get it out immediately and repair the damage, or he'll bleed to death." Looking up at the threatening clouds, he added, "We'd better get him to the stage before it starts to pour."

Cradling the wounded man in his arms, the rangy lawman carried him back to the stagecoach and, under the doctor's direction, laid him on one of the seats.

As the man was beginning to regain consciousness, Dr. Simms asked McKee, "What's his name?"

"Trowbridge," McKee responded. "Al Trowbridge."

The sky was now covered with heavy black clouds, and the wind was blowing hard. Shouting against the wind, Suzanne said, "I'll help if you need me, Doctor."

As he ripped the torn shirt away from the wound, Simms yelled, "Good, Mrs. Lane. First, ask Bates if there's any whiskey on the stage."

When Suzanne returned less than a minute later with a full bottle, Simms was explaining to the wounded man who he was and what he was about to do. Trowbridge nodded weakly that he understood.

"Get as much whiskey in him as you can," Simms said to Suzanne. "He's losing blood fast. There isn't much time."

While she began to pour whiskey down the bleeding man's throat, the doctor wiped clean the area around the bullet hole.

Sid Bingham suddenly stuck his head inside the stage and declared, "Hey, Doc. Take a look up at that sky. Maybe you'd better hold off removin' the bullet right now so we can hightail it out of here and find some shelter. I've seen clouds like these before; they spawn tornadoes."

Shaking his head, Simms replied, "There's no time. The

man will die if I don't get the bullet out and stop the bleeding. And even if I do, his chances aren't so good."

Bingham swore and said, "But we could *all* die if we don't get out of here, Simms!"

The marshal laid a firm hand on the gunfighter's shoulder and said above the howl of the wind, "Back off, Bingham. Let the doctor do his job."

Bingham turned to face the marshal, and the look in his eyes clearly announced a challenge, but it quickly faded. Shrugging his shoulders, he quietly stepped away from the coach.

Dr. Simms smiled reassuringly at Suzanne as they waited a few more minutes for the whiskey to take effect. When he was sure it had, he carefully began probing for the slug in the man's stomach.

Pearl Madison suddenly grasped her husband's arm and pointed to the southwest. "Ollie!" she gasped, terror in her eyes. "Look!"

Everyone outside the coach followed the direction of Pearl's finger. A huge black funnel was swooping toward them from the angry, churning sky.

# Chapter Seven

Lightning slashed the ebony sky and thunder boomed as Dr. Burke Simms hurriedly stitched up the wound of Al Trowbridge, who had slipped into unconsciousness again during the surgery. Simms looked out over his shoulder. Through the haze of dust permeating the air, he could just make out the black, twisting funnel that was almost touching the ground, drawing dangerously near the horrified passengers and crew of the stagecoach.

Floyd Bates leaned inside the coach, looked weakly at Suzanne and the doctor, and said in a strained voice, "Doc, that funnel is comin' right for us! We've got to get out of here fast!"

Oliver Madison, looking extremely agitated, peered in through the window on the other side. There was desperation in his voice as he said, "Doctor, please don't endanger the lives of all the rest of us for the sake of tending to this one man! If anything were to happen to Pearl . . ."

Making the final stitches, Simms said over his shoulder, "All right, Mr. Madison. I'm just about finished."

The air was filled with the horrible roaring of the approaching tornado, and the horses began whinnying wildly

"Hang on, Al!" McKee yelled to his still-unconscious friend. "Don't quit on me yet! We're gonna get through this, you'll see!"

Burke Simms struggled on behind Gunnison and McKee. He suddenly stumbled and fell, and Suzanne hurried to help him to his feet.

"Dr. Simms!" she hollered. "Here, grab my hand!"

"No!" he shouted to her. "You go on! I don't want to slow you down."

"Well, I'm not leaving without you." She assisted the elderly physician to his feet and helped steady him as they pushed their way through the thrashing grass.

Sid Bingham held his hat clamped to his head as he battled his way through the lashing wind to reach the relative safety of the ravine. When he saw Simms fall, the gunfighter ignored the physician's plight. *Doc's already caused enough trouble,* Bingham told himself. *If he hadn't insisted on helping that drifter, we'd all be safe right now!*

As the passengers reached the ravine and climbed down into it, they flattened on the ground. Oliver Madison placed his arm protectively across his wife's prone body, shouting over and over, "We'll be all right, Pearl. Don't worry. We'll be all right. . . ."

Marshal Gunnison rested Al Trowbridge against the leeward wall of the dried-up riverbed, and then he hurried over to Suzanne Lane. He held her tightly as they lay in the sand with their faces buried in their arms while the storm raged overhead.

Suzanne had never been so frightened in her life. It felt as if the end of the world were at hand. She began to whimper, wishing she had never made this foolish journey. Even if she had found Johnny Valentine before the Decker gang, would the revenge of taking his life have been worth losing her own?

It seemed like an eternity before the deafening roar let

up slightly in its intensity. One by one, the passengers cautiously lifted their heads, squinting against the dirt that had been whipped up by the wind and was now pelting their faces.

Sid Bingham stood up, then yelled, "Look!" He pointed off to the east. "It veered off and missed us! Hah!" He started to climb back out when the roaring wind grew louder again. Pivoting around, he saw the second tornado bearing down, heading straight for the stagecoach.

At the coach Floyd Bates was still swearing and fighting his frenzied team. At the renewed roar, he shifted in his seat and looked back. He stiffened like a statue, paralyzed by the sight. When Sam Todd saw the howling black funnel drawing closer, he stood up to leap from his seat, but it was too late. Both stagecoach and team suddenly disappeared as the dark, swirling mass swallowed everything up in a deadly roar.

The fury of the storm was completely unleashed. Gunnison hurled himself on top of Suzanne, covering her with his body. A darkness like midnight surrounded them, and the howling of the wind was so loud that they thought their eardrums would burst. Gunnison felt as though the air were being sucked from his body, and he had trouble breathing. He pressed closer to Suzanne, trying to shelter her as best he could.

Pearl Madison screamed, but her screams were drowned out by the tornado's roar. Then, after what seemed an eternity, the terrible fury ended and a measure of light returned as the tornado lifted skyward and roared away on its destructive journey.

Then without warning parts of the stagecoach began raining down from the sky. One of the stagecoach's wheels came whistling down, striking the marshal's left calf, and Gunnison howled in pain as he rolled off Suzanne.

Suzanne raised her head in time to see the wheel spin a

few feet and flop to the ground. "Dr. Simms!" she yelled. "Marshal Gunnison is hurt!"

Burke Simms lifted himself into a sitting position. He brushed the sand off his face and out of his silver hair, then wiped his hands on the front of his frock coat. "Okay," he said. "Let me take a look."

With the worst of the danger finally over, the able-bodied passengers stood and looked around. The sky was now a normal leaden gray, and lightning lanced overhead accompanied by the heavy rumble of thunder. It was starting to rain.

Pearl Madison suddenly giggled, giddy with relief. Then she put her hand to her mouth, flustered and embarrassed, and said to Suzanne, "Oh, dear! I hope you don't think I'm laughing at Marshal Gunnison."

"Not at all, Pearl. I understand," the redhead assured her with a slight smile, although worry was creasing her brow.

The group gathered around Gunnison as Simms made a quick examination of the lawman's leg. Clenching his teeth, the marshal grimaced in pain.

"How bad is it?" asked Suzanne.

The physician shook his head. "It's definitely fractured. I'm going to have to set it."

"Doc," spoke up Sid Bingham, "is there anything I can do to help?"

"Yes, there is," answered Simms, noticing that Suzanne was as startled as he was at Bingham's unexpected concern. "See if you and the other men can find some pieces of the stagecoach that can be used as splints. And maybe some others that will work as crutches." He looked over to where the stagecoach had been. "I'm afraid there's only one way we're going to get any farther, and that's to walk, and the only chance the marshal will have to do that is with crutches."

Madison, McKee, and Bingham began to walk across the area, searching for usable parts of the stagecoach. Their stomachs wrenched when they saw the bloody remains of the horses scattered about. There were no signs of the driver and shotgunner, and the three men were grateful for that.

The physician looked glumly at the marshal. "I hate to be the bearer of more bad tidings, but setting your leg is not going to be a very pleasant experience. I don't even have anything to give you to relieve the pain, since the bottle of whiskey was on the stage."

Suzanne knelt beside the injured lawman. She had the unseemly desire to reach out and take hold of his hand to comfort him, but she fought the urge. She looked up at Pearl Madison, then asked the doctor, "What can we do to help, Dr. Simms?"

The doctor thought a moment. Looking first at his patient and then at the women, he said, "I'll tell you what, ladies. It actually would be less distracting for me to do my job if you were to take yourselves off a ways. You see, the marshal's going to experience a great deal of pain, and it would probably be easier for him to be able to swear and cuss without having to worry about offending your delicate sensibilities. And that would be one less thing *I* would have to worry about."

Pearl blushed. "I must admit, that would be fine with me, Dr. Simms. To tell you the truth, I'm feeling a bit faint anyway, and the thought of Marshal Gunnison experiencing all that pain . . . Excuse me—" she said suddenly, and hurried off.

Suzanne began to protest. "I won't be offended, Dr. Simms, I assure you. I—"

"Dr. Simms is right, Mrs. Lane," Gunnison put in. "I appreciate your kindness, but I would feel better if you do as he suggests."

"I'll signal you when I'm done," Simms said.

"Of course, Doctor," Suzanne said. "I understand." As she was getting up, she leaned over and impulsively kissed the lawman lightly on the lips. Then she walked quickly to where Pearl Madison sat with her head bent, some thirty feet away.

Overwhelmed by Suzanne's action, the marshal felt his heart beat rapidly, and for a moment he forgot his injury. Then a sharp stab of pain brought him back to reality. He looked over at the unconscious Al Trowbridge, then at the elderly physician, and said softly, "That was very smoothly done, you old sidewinder. It's only because I *know* what it is you really want to talk about that I could see through you."

Kneeling down, the physician also spoke quietly. "Well, Johnny Valentine, I was going to try one more time to persuade you to give up your pursuit of the Decker gang, but now perhaps I won't have to. This broken leg is going to be more persuasive than I could ever be. I know catching those outlaws is the only thing you can think about, but you're just going to have to forget it."

"How can you even suggest such a thing, Doc?" asked the sandy-haired man, grimacing. "Don't forget, that was my kid brother Decker gunned down at the Silver Saddle. This busted leg may postpone my going after Decker, but I still intend to track him and his whole bunch down. Believe me, they're going to pay for murdering Jim."

"Johnny, listen to me," pleaded Simms, looking around to make sure the others were still far enough away not to overhear. "Why not let the federal men handle it? After all, Decker and his men killed Ford Gunnison, too. There'll be swarms of U.S. marshals combing this part of the country looking for Decker."

"Doc, as long as I live, I'll never forget the sight of Jim's bullet-riddled body. When I rode into Dodge and saw who it was you were leaning over, I felt as though a piece of my heart had been ripped out of my chest."

"I know you did, son," Simms said compassionately. "You know, I hadn't seen you in years, but you and Jim looked so much alike that the minute I saw you standing there, I knew who you were—even with that long hair and mustache you had taken to wearing."

"Yeah," the gunfighter said bitterly, "it was his looking like me that got Jim murdered. Well, Decker's gonna be mighty sorry he made a mistake and killed the wrong Valentine."

"Well, I'm mighty sorry I couldn't talk you out of this harebrained scheme you came up with. I don't know why the town council agreed to go along with it." Simms sniffed and added wryly, "I'm not sure it's such a good idea to have you playing the part of Marshal Gunnison, a dead man. Even if it does result in the Decker gang's capture."

"Now, Doc, I think we worked out a fine arrangement. To tell you the truth, I've always hated the kind of life I've led as a gunfighter, and I've wanted to find a way out of it. When I got word of the inheritance from my father's estate, I planned on buying a small spread near Dodge, to be close to my family once again. . . ." The pain written on Valentine's face was as much from his brother's and sister's deaths as from his fractured leg. "Well, my family's gone. . . . I don't know what your beef is, Doc. The town council was unanimous about letting me take on Gunnison's identity when we held that secret meeting, and you know I'll drop the disguise as soon as Decker's been arrested."

The elderly physician shook his head. "My beef, as you put it, is that I want to see you stay alive, you darn fool—although I must say, I was surprised that everything went so smoothly. You and the bartender whisked the bodies to my office so quickly that I don't think anyone else in town—other than the council members and the undertaker, of course—even realized Gunnison was dead, not just wounded, or that it was Jim who was killed, not you." Simms sighed. "Maybe you're right. Maybe it *is* fate."

Valentine grinned despite his pain. "And maybe it was fate that put Danny Wellman in front of me with a loaded gun in his hand in the first place. If it hadn't been for Wellman, I wouldn't have met Suzanne Lane, now, would I?"

Simms scratched his head.

"And was it also just coincidence that you were planning to make this trip to Salina, putting you on the same stage with me to be here to take care of my leg so I can keep up my search?"

"Now, come on, John—I mean, Ford." Simms looked around cautiously. "You're taking this fate thing too far. And listen to me, son. As far as getting any closer to Mrs. Lane, you're playing with dynamite there. You'd better quit your involvement with her right now. Have you thought of what it would do to her to find out you're the man who killed her husband? I know it was unavoidable, but the widow Lane might feel a whole lot differently."

Valentine looked pensive. "I hate deceiving her, Doc, and I sure never planned to. But she's going home to Great Bend, and I'm going to keep moving. She won't ever know."

"Then in the name of all that's decent, don't start romancing her," urged Simms. "She's a wonderful woman, and she deserves better than that."

Valentine looked contrite. "You're right, Doc," he said with a sigh, but he knew that in Suzanne's presence he would find it awfully hard to squelch his feelings. He was falling head over heels in love with her—and he could tell by the way she looked at him that she felt the same way. Of course, he knew that her husband had been carrying on with Emma—and that made him dead sure that the Lanes had not had a real marriage for a long time.

Then he reminded himself that Suzanne Lane knew him as U.S. Marshal Ford Gunnison—not as the gunfighter Johnny Valentine. Once she found out that he was an impostor and learned who he really was, she would hate him with a passion stronger than any fond feelings that were growing between them. . . .

He shifted his body uneasily, and he had to grind his teeth against the pain in his leg. He would not let things between them grow any stronger, he vowed to himself. He would be out of her life as soon as possible anyway, to get back on Decker's trail.

"I hope the federal men don't find Decker," Valentine said to the doctor through clenched teeth. "I want him. I want him real bad."

"Be reasonable," Simms answered. "The gang's too big. There's no way you can take them all on without getting yourself killed."

"That'll be my worry, Doc," grunted Valentine. "Your worry is to set my leg. Why don't you get to it?"

"Okay, but I wasn't kidding, son, when I said it's going to hurt. You just be prepared for it. Here, bite down on this."

He gave Valentine a wadded handkerchief to put between his teeth. Then, taking the broken leg in both hands, he snapped the bones into place.

The gunfighter's teeth dug deeply into the cloth as the pain shot up his leg and exploded throughout his body. Then the pain faded into a gray fog, and he fell into unconsciousness.

Tender hands were dabbing the raindrops and beads of sweat from his face as Johnny Valentine came to. A soft voice asked anxiously, "Ford, are you in much pain?"

Valentine blinked against the rain and opened his eyes to see Suzanne Lane's lovely face peering down at him, and he realized his head was cradled in her lap. Suddenly he understood. He had passed out when Doc Simms set his broken leg. He had a vague memory of terrible pain, but that had diminished, and all he felt now was a steady, dull throbbing.

"It's not too bad," he answered her. "Thanks for your concern."

"My pleasure," she said, smiling warmly.

Valentine hated to leave Suzanne's lap, but he forced himself into a sitting position. He found that his leg was in a tight splint made from spokes from a stagecoach wheel wrapped with cotton strips, which he guessed had come from Suzanne's petticoat.

Sid Bingham stepped up and handed him a crude set of crutches, made from the crotches of two branches. "These ain't too fancy, Marshal, but maybe they'll help you get along."

Valentine's suspicions were aroused. Why was Bingham suddenly so concerned about him? Perhaps the man recognized that they all needed each other if they were to reach civilization safely, and he did not want to antagonize anyone. Valentine mentally shrugged and let Bingham and Suzanne help him to his feet.

The lightning and thunder were easing off, but the wind was picking up and the rain was beginning to fall harder. It was difficult to distinguish between the groans of Al Trowbridge—conscious now and lying on a litter that Oliver Madison and Gene McKee had made from sections of the stagecoach—and the moaning wind.

Burke Simms raised his voice to be heard by the group. "Best I can figure, we're about halfway between Larned and Pawnee Rock—maybe a mite closer to Pawnee Rock. It'll still be a good five miles, but I suggest that we head that way. It'll be slow going, what with the marshal on crutches and Trowbridge needing to be carried on his litter, but we can't stay here. We need to get shelter and food and water."

Everyone agreed, and with the rain lashing them the small group headed northeast toward the town of Pawnee Rock.

The winding Arkansas River came into view off to their right, its rising waters churning from the heavy downpour of rain. The journey was slow and hard in the rain and mud, and the travelers weakened as night came on. They had gone only a little over two miles when Pearl Madison wiped her eyes and pointed ahead.

"Look, a farmhouse!" she shouted.

The others peered through the gathering gloom and the heavy rain. The dark dwelling looked deserted, but the sight of the old house was a welcome one.

"Good!" exclaimed the physician. "At least we'll be sheltered for the night."

Because they had to move so slowly, it took them almost a half hour to reach the farmhouse, and by then darkness had settled in, obscuring the way. But they could clearly hear the roar of the turbid Arkansas River, and they followed it until they could make out the vague form of the porch. Sid Bingham rushed ahead of the others and tried the door. It was unlocked.

Everyone filed into the house, glad at last to get out of the rain, since they were all soaked through to the skin. Of course, a deserted house meant that no food would be had that evening, but its shelter would at least enable them to dry off. It was as much as they could hope for. By morning perhaps the rain would have stopped, making the rest of the journey easier.

Bingham tried lighting his matches, but they were too

wet. Everyone fumbled his way around the dark rooms of the house, hoping to find matches and, with luck, an oil lamp or a candle—or anything usable that might have been left behind by the former occupants. They came up with nothing.

Bone-tired, the group finally stretched out on the floor of the one room that did not seem to have any leaks from the roof.

Johnny Valentine's leg was hurting again, and he found that by sitting up the pain was lessened. Periodically the room would be illuminated by a bright flash of lightning, enabling him to look at his fellow refugees—particularly at Suzanne, who was sitting up beside him, her damp hair curling on her creamy brow in a most provocative manner.

Desire quickened within him. He wanted to take the beautiful creature in his arms and kiss her. He wanted to tell her of his feelings for her, that he found her captivating and irresistible. But while his heart wanted Suzanne Lane for his own, his mind scolded him for such thoughts, reminding him he had to get out of her life before she found out who he really was. She would surely hate him then—no matter how unhappy her marriage had been.

Struggling to squelch his desire for her, he said, "Suzanne, you're tired. Lie down now and get some sleep."

But leaning toward him, she shook her head and whispered, "Not just yet. I—I wanted to say something to you first." She paused for a moment, then whispered even softer, "You must think I'm some kind of heartless hussy."

"What do you mean?"

"You heard me say that my husband was killed only a few days ago. For me to kiss you with Frank barely cold in his grave, you must think—"

"Suzanne, what I think is that your marriage must not have been the best," Valentine said truthfully.

The redheaded woman sighed deeply. She wanted to

tell the U.S. marshal she had feelings for him that she had never had for Frank; instead, she began to tell him about her marriage. "I appreciate your speaking your mind, and it's true: The love had slipped out of our marriage. I . . . I thought it was a good marriage, and at first it was. But in the last year or so, it had begun to deteriorate. I thought perhaps we could pull it back together, make it as good as it used to be, but it never happened. We seemed to grow farther and farther apart, and my husband seemed to need me less and less." She paused for a moment, then said somewhat shyly, "I'm glad you don't think less of me, and I want you to know that I would never have been so disloyal to Frank's memory if . . . if—"

"I don't think you were being disloyal at all. What I do think is that your husband was a fool to put anything—or anyone—before you," Valentine said more vehemently than he had intended. Lowering his voice, he asked, "Do you think there was another woman in your husband's life?"

"No, I'm sure there wasn't. Frank was just completely wrapped up with the business. His only passion was making money."

Valentine knew differently and decided to move on to another subject. "What will you do now? Will you take over the business, now that Frank is gone?"

"I've hired a man to oversee the stores—that's how I was able to get away on this trip—and I will be able to live well off my share of the profits. Beyond that, I haven't really given any thought to what I'll be doing, or where, for that matter."

"Do you think you'll marry again? Oh, I'm sorry," Valentine put in immediately. "That was unfeeling of me. As you said, your husband just died."

"It's all right. I don't mind your asking," Suzanne replied. "I suppose I will marry again—if the right man asks me. And if . . . if I can get this hatred for Johnny Valentine out of my heart. Even though he's dead, I can't stop hating him for robbing me of the chance to make things better between Frank and me. And if I don't get rid of the hatred, it will dry me up inside." She began to weep softly.

Though it pained him to move, Valentine reached out in the dark and pulled Suzanne to him. Her head against his shoulder, her muffled cries tore at his heart, and without thinking, he kissed her head and stroked her hair, trying to comfort her.

Abruptly she withdrew her head from his shoulder, and in a flash of lightning he could see her face turned toward his.

"Suzanne, I apologize. I didn't mean to offend you. It's just that I've never felt so comfortable with a woman in my life as I do with you."

"Oh, Ford, you *didn't* offend me. I was thinking the very same thing. I—"

He cut off her words with a tender kiss. They pulled apart briefly, then kissed again, and Valentine felt as though he were on fire. He wanted this beautiful woman more than he had ever wanted anyone . . . but he reminded himself that she could never be his. He would see her safely to Pawnee Rock; then he would buy a horse and ride out of her life forever.

"You had better get some rest now," he said as he reluctantly parted from her embrace. "It's going to be a long, hard walk in the mud tomorrow till we reach Pawnee Rock."

"You're right," she said, settling down beside him. "Are you going to be able to sleep?"

"I think so," he lied. "As long as I stay in this position, the pain's almost unnoticeable."

Accepting his word for it, Suzanne lay down beside

him, and within minutes her breathing fell into a steady rhythm. Valentine noticed that the rain had ceased to be the dominant sound, the roar of the Arkansas River now surpassing it. If they were lucky, the sun would be shining in the morning; if they were very lucky, they would make it to Pawnee Rock without incident.

The impostor began to think about the Indian problem at hand. Nobody had voiced any fears, but he was sure they all were aware of the danger. If the Kiowa camp was close enough for three of the renegades to have attacked Trowbridge and McKee, an entire war party might attack them tomorrow. The sound of the rain on the roof was now very light. Valentine decided that maybe just one man should go for help while the rest of them remained out of sight in this old house. If they were all caught out in the open by the Kiowas, they would not have a chance.

Another flash of lightning brightened the room, and Valentine saw that Sid Bingham was sitting up and watching him. When the light was gone, the gunfighter's cynical voice cut through the darkness. "It's real nice to see that you are such a comfort to the widow, Marshal. That was a touching scene."

Valentine felt his temper rise. "It's none of your business, Bingham!"

"You made it *your* business to tell me to quit lookin' at her," retorted Bingham. "I sure never kissed her."

Valentine looked down at Suzanne's dark form lying next to him and was glad that she was asleep. Looking back at the silhouetted form of the gunfighter, he retorted, "If your eyesight's so good, then you could easily see that the lady wanted my attentions. I didn't force myself on her."

He paused, shifted slightly against the wall, and changing the subject, asked, "Where you bound for, anyway, Bingham?"

"Abilene," came the flat answer.

"Are you looking to challenge someone there?"

"Yep." After a brief pause, Bingham said, "Word has it Bill Pearce is in Abilene."

"Bill Pearce?" Valentine gasped. "I hope you're joking."

"I don't joke about gunfightin', Gunnison."

"You're a fool if you go up against the likes of him. The man is lightning fast and deadly with that iron on his hip."

"I'm faster and I'm deadlier!"

"A lot of men have thought that," came Valentine's hasty reply. "They're in their graves, and Pearce is still breathing."

"He won't be when I get through with him."

"I wish you luck, Bingham. It'd be too bad if you survived a tornado just to end up dead by your own choice."

Bingham was quiet for a moment. Then he said, "Too bad Johnny Valentine got himself ambushed by the Decker gang. I had plans to go after him once I'd put Pearce down."

"Valentine, huh?" said the impostor. "Bingham, you're a dreamer. Johnny Valentine would have left you with your hand on the gun butt, the gun still in its holster."

Bingham chuckled. "You're wrong, Gunnison. I could have taken Valentine. But I guess I'll never be able to prove it now, will I?"

"Be a bit difficult."

"Yeah," agreed Bingham sardonically, "it'd be a bit difficult."

# Chapter Eight

Johnny Valentine opened his eyes the next morning and looked out to see clouds still hanging in the Kansas sky. The rain had stopped, but the roar of the Arkansas River had replaced it. Rising unsteadily to his feet, he used the crude crutches to make his way to the back windows. As he watched the rushing, muddy river for a few moments, he realized it was near to overflowing its banks. If it did, it could sweep away the old farmhouse. His plan of having one man go to Pawnee Rock would have to be scrapped.

Valentine walked over to Burke Simms, who was tending Al Trowbridge. "How's he doing, Doc?" he asked.

"Better than I would have thought, with such a serious wound," the physician replied. "And how are you doing, Marshal?"

"Also better than you would have thought. I heal fast, Doc." He leaned down and said to the wounded man, "I was hoping one of us could go for help while the rest of us stayed put, but the way that river's rising, we'd all better get out of here soon. Do you think you can make it okay?"

"Sure, Marshal," Trowbridge answered. "I'll be ridin', after all. The rest of you will have to walk."

The sun was breaking through the clouds when the exhausted group reached the outskirts of Pawnee Rock, with Sid Bingham and Oliver Madison carrying a make-shift litter on which Al Trowbridge lay. It was just shy of noon, and the travelers plodded with renewed vigor through the last quarter mile of the ankle-deep muck, which had been a road the day before.

"Even stale bread would taste like a banquet at this point, I do believe," Pearl Madison declared.

"You said it, Mrs. Madison," Gene McKee agreed. "You know, I've always hated cold mutton soup, but if somebody were to offer me a bowl right now, I'd finish it and ask for seconds."

Everyone laughed, giddy at the thought that their arduous journey was finally over.

They had gotten within a hundred yards of the town when Johnny Valentine suddenly hobbled to the forefront of the group and held up his hand for them to stop.

"What's the matter, Marshal?" Oliver Madison asked.

"Something's not right here. It's too quiet."

The group stood staring at the main street of the small town. The only sounds they heard were the soft wind through the trees and, somewhere far off, the mournful howling of a dog. Everybody had the same thought, but nobody wanted to say it aloud: Indians.

Slowly they proceeded forward. Minutes later they stopped dead in their tracks, shocked. Bodies were strewn everywhere—on porches, in yards, in the street. At the very first house in town, the body of a woman riddled with arrows was draped over a porch railing, a livid red patch on her head where her hair had been.

Pearl gasped and threw a hand to her mouth, trying not to be sick.

"Kiowas!" blurted Gene McKee, his face losing color, and he looked at his wounded friend.

"Oh, dear God, no!" prayed Suzanne, clutching at Valentine's arm.

"We'd better be real careful. Those renegades might still be around."

Gene McKee walked up to Valentine. "Marshal, let me go search the town. If anyone's alive, they might need Doc's help, and it'd be quicker for one or two of us to go lookin' instead of all of us. If them Indians are still in town, the whole group would be a lot more conspicuous. No offense, Marshal, but you ain't exactly nimble-footed right now, so it'll be best if you stay with Doc and the ladies and Al here and get inside that house."

"He's right. I'll go with him," Bingham volunteered, and he and Madison gently set the litter on the ground.

Johnny Valentine handed McKee his gun. "Take this with you, just in case."

McKee accepted the weapon, and he and Bingham cautiously headed up the street.

With Dr. Simms and Madison carrying the litter, the rest of the group hurried inside the house, looking away from the body of the woman. Dr. Simms put his hand on Valentine's arm and said, "Marshal, I don't think you can go any farther on foot. We'll have to find some other way to get you to Great Bend. No doubt the Kiowas have taken all the horses from the town but maybe we can find a buggy to put you and Trowbridge in—and the women, too. Worse comes to worst, we'll *pull* it to Great Bend."

Outside in the unearthly quiet of the street, McKee and Bingham, their weapons ready, entered house after house but found only corpses. The two men had worked their way to the east end of the small town and had rounded the corner of a house when suddenly a rifle cracked, chewing wood where Gene McKee's head had been a second before. Both men whirled and dived back around the corner as a second rifle roared, splintering more wood.

"It's comin' from that stone barn across the way!" gasped McKee, flattening himself against the wall next to Bingham. "Must be people there."

"Yeah," said Bingham, holding his gun ready, "but are they red or white?"

McKee thought over the situation, then declared, "Must be survivors. They wouldn't be hidin' if they were the Indians. They're probably so spooked, they didn't even notice we weren't Kiowas. They're just shootin' at anything that moves."

"I expect you're right," agreed Bingham. "I think I'll let 'em know who we are." Inching his way to the edge of the house, he cupped his hands around his mouth and shouted, "Hey, you in the barn! We're not Kiowas! We're white men! We're friends! Don't shoot!"

A male voice came from the barn. "Step out where I can see you!"

"My name is Sid Bingham and the man with me is Gene McKee. There are six others with us. We were on a stagecoach yesterday, heading for Great Bend, when a tornado hit our coach and destroyed it. We're all on foot."

"Come on out!" called the man in the barn. "I won't shoot at you again."

Bingham peered cautiously around the corner, getting a good look at the barn. Made of stone, the impressive structure might originally have been made to double as a fortress, he thought, to be used as it had been today. The roof was made out of sod, and the windows were covered by heavy shutters, with thin slots in them so that guns could be fired in relative safety from inside the barn.

Stepping around the corner of the house, Bingham said to McKee, "C'mon."

As soon as the two men showed themselves, the barn door opened, and a short, stocky, broad-shouldered man with black, curly hair stepped out, rifle in hand. He looked to be in his late thirties. He smiled as Bingham and McKee walked toward him.

"I'm Paul Warrick," he said, extending his hand.

Bingham identified himself as he shook the offered hand.

"Then you must be McKee," Warrick said as he shook hands with the other man. "Is that another of your party?" he asked, pointing behind the two men.

Both men turned and saw Oliver Madison standing at the corner of the house where they had been a few moments earlier.

"We heard gunshots!" Madison called. "Is everything all right?"

"Yeah!" replied Bingham. "Bring the others over here to the barn." When Madison nodded and disappeared around the corner, Bingham turned back to Warrick and asked, "How many of you are in there?"

"Five, including myself," responded the worn and haggard-looking man. "Trailing-the-Enemy and his bunch hit us just after sunup this morning. I don't think they left anyone else in town alive."

"We couldn't find anyone," McKee confirmed, shaking his head sadly.

Warrick heard the barn door squeak behind him. Turning, he said, "Come on out. Everything's all right. These men are friends."

The four other survivors of the massacre emerged from inside the barn. Warrick put his arm around a slender, attractive woman who stood an inch taller than he. "This is my wife, Doreen."

"Hello," she said somewhat nervously, running a hand

through her straggly brown hair while holding her other hand to her left eye.

A handsome, slim young man named Stuart Vance was introduced next, followed by a petite, blond young woman named Marianna Freeman. Jason Hart, Marianna's widower uncle with whom she lived, was the final survivor to be introduced. The graying Hart kept a watchful eye on his pretty ward.

Gene McKee looked at Doreen Warrick and asked, "Did something happen to your eye, ma'am?"

"Yes. When Paul and I were trying to make it here to the barn, I peeked around the corner of a house just as a Kiowa fired his rifle. The bullet chewed into the wood, and splinters flew into my eye."

"Well, you're in luck, ma'am. We've got a doctor with us."

"Oh, thank goodness!" exclaimed Doreen. "The pain's just terrible! I—"

"Did I hear someone say they need a doctor?"

Everyone turned at the sound of Burke Simms's voice. Paul Warrick looked at the newcomers, then said to Bingham, "I take it this is the rest of your group." Looking back at them, he said, "My name is Paul Warrick. I was just telling your friends who we are and how we survived the raid this morning."

Simms, who along with Oliver Madison was supporting Al Trowbridge on the litter, introduced himself and the rest of his own group of survivors.

"My wife can certainly use your help, Doc," Warrick said. He looked at Gene McKee and suggested, "Perhaps you can relieve the doctor of his burden. Why don't you take your wounded Mr. Trowbridge into the barn. It looks to me as though he needs some rest."

"I'll get him settled," Pearl volunteered.

Suzanne Lane suggested, "Perhaps I can help you with

Mrs. Warrick, Dr. Simms. I seem to be getting quite proficient at nursing."

Simms smiled and said, "That you are, Mrs. Lane. Thank you, I accept your offer. You can hand me my instruments as I ask for them, if you will. Why don't we go over by the barn ourselves? It might be best if Mrs. Warrick has something to lean up against. It would help keep her head steady while I work."

Paul Warrick watched his wife be led over to the barn. Then he turned around and smiled at Johnny Valentine. Reading the badge pinned to the impostor's chest, he declared, "Well, Marshal, it's good to have a lawman with us, even if you aren't in the best of health. Did your leg get broken during your tussle with the tornado?"

Valentine smiled in return, nodding his head. "I'm afraid so. Tell me, Mr. Warrick, why haven't you moved back to your homes yet?"

"Because I don't think we've seen the last of the renegades, Marshal," Warrick said flatly. "We reached the barn by the grace of God, and I think it would be most unwise to leave it just yet. As you can see, it's virtually a fort."

"You really think the Indians will be back?" Valentine asked.

Warrick ran his hand over his mouth. "I'm sure of it. The Kiowas surrounded the barn for an hour, and then they left. When they did, we ran to some of the nearby houses and grabbed up guns and ammunition, to be on the safe side. We also grabbed more food and water. Just as we feared, they came back to hit us a second time. We held them off again, and they left again—but Trailing-the-Enemy isn't going to let us live if he can help it." He stopped and shook his head sadly. "Jason, Stuart, and I were about to start burying our dead when you people showed up."

Marianna Freeman suddenly walked away from her uncle and stepped up close to Sid Bingham, eyeing him with admiration. Her full red lips formed a provocative smile as she said, "Did I hear you say your name is Sid Bingham? Are you the famous Sid Bingham, the gunfighter?"

Bingham smirked. "That's me."

"How many men have you killed, Mr. Bingham?"

"Really, Marianna," Jason Hart scolded, folding his arms sternly across his ample potbelly. "You shouldn't ask those kind of questions."

"Oh, pshaw, Uncle Jason," she said, flipping a hand at him. She turned back to Bingham and breathed softly, "You don't mind telling someone how many men you've killed, do you, Mr. Bingham?"

The gunfighter grinned crookedly and said, "Not when that someone is as pretty as you, Marianna. Let's see, so far, I've put fourteen men in the sod. And you can call me Sid."

Stuart Vance's face looked as though he had just smelled something strong and repugnant, and his color deepened, starting at the base of his neck and working up into his face. Bingham saw the youth's reaction but ignored him. He had a good dozen years of experience and at least forty pounds on Vance.

Marianna smiled and laced her fingers together. "Thank you, Sid," she said. Tilting her head coyly, she remarked, "A gunfighter's life must really be exciting. I guess you must be a real he-man."

"Marianna!" Jason Hart said angrily. "You never would have said such things if your aunt were still alive. This is no kind of talk for a girl of eighteen! And besides, we've suffered a terrible tragedy here today. Have you no respect for the dead?" Hart suddenly looked around, and his face colored. "Forgive me, everyone. I didn't mean to air our differences in public. Marianna, I want you to get

some food together. These folks must be starving if they
haven't eaten since yesterday. Go on, girl!"

"I'll give you a hand, little lady," Bingham said.

Stuart Vance stepped between Bingham and Marianna,
staring coldly at the gunfighter. "She doesn't need your
help, mister. Leave her alone!"

Before the gunfighter could respond to young Vance's
outburst, Johnny Valentine grabbed Bingham's shoulder
and snapped, "Back off!"

"Now, look, Gunnison!" rasped Bingham, shaking off
the hand. "You've got no call to order me about. Besides,"
he said, feigning innocence, "I was only trying to be
helpful to the lady."

"I'm warning you, Bingham. These two young people
obviously mean something to each other. You're just passing through, so quit interfering in their lives!"

"That's right!" Vance declared, enjoying the reprimand
the gunfighter received. "Marianna's my girl!" He smiled,
satisfied that the matter was settled.

The flirtatious young blonde, however, found the attentions of the well-known gunfighter quite enjoyable. For
the moment she decided to do her uncle's bidding, but
she was not going to let such an opportunity pass her by
for long. With a toss of her blond hair she went back
inside the barn.

Valentine watched Bingham and Vance carefully until
he was sure the two combatants had calmed down. Then
he asked Paul Warrick about their provisions.

"Well, we have plenty of guns and ammunition—we've
gathered handguns and rifles from all the nearest houses—
and there's probably enough food and water in the houses
and the general store to keep us going for weeks."

Valentine frowned. "I certainly hope that won't be necessary. Tell me, Mr. Warrick, are there any horses left, or
did the Kiowas take them all?"

"I'm afraid they took them all. The wagons, too."

"Well, as long as there are plenty of supplies, the best thing we can do is wait to be rescued. Our stagecoach was due to arrive in Great Bend last night, so by now the Butterfield company knows something's happened to us. They've probably already sent out a rescue party, figuring we must have met up with the storm. I guess for the time being we should eat and rest up a bit. Then we can all make forays over to the houses and the store for more food and water."

"I agree, Marshal," Warrick said. "The living have to come before the dead. Perhaps in the morning we can dig a common grave for all those poor souls the Kiowas massacred. Right now we need to recoup our strength."

Everyone went into the stone barn, and as an extra precaution the big barn door was locked and barricaded. The shutters on the two windows were left unlatched, and young Paul Warrick was posted by them as a lookout. Four oil lanterns provided additional light inside the barn. The occupants sat clustered on boxes and small wooden kegs to partake of the food that Doreen and Marianna had prepared. The exception was Al Trowbridge, who lay on the floor, his head propped against a keg as he awkwardly attempted to eat.

During the meal the men discussed what they knew of the renegade Kiowas. Gene McKee suggested, "Maybe the smartest thing for us to do is head for Great Bend tonight, under cover of darkness."

"How would we go?" asked Jason Hart. "Without horses, it would take hours, and we'd be out in the open come daybreak. Trailing-the-Enemy would love to catch us like that."

McKee hunched his shoulders and sighed. "Guess you're

right. I just hate waiting around for them Indians to come back."

While the other men talked, Sid Bingham sat silently looking at Marianna Freeman. Their eyes locked from time to time, and she smiled furtively, unaware that Stuart Vance was watching.

Vance finally had all he could take. Setting his food on the floor, he leaped off the keg he had been sitting on and stomped angrily over to the young woman. "Marianna, that gunfighter doesn't care anything about you, only that you're pretty and female. You're making a fool of yourself!"

The young woman tried to control her temper. "Stuart, I did not ask you for your opinion. You're a good friend, and I'm very fond of you, but you're overstepping your bounds. I'll be nice to Sid if I wish, and if he wants to be nice to me, I shall welcome his attentions."

Johnny Valentine had had enough. Hoisting himself up on his crutches, he hobbled over to the young woman. "Look, Marianna," he said, "whether you care to admit it or not, you are very young. Bingham's been around, and he's pretty quick to show some attention to a woman. Quit playing with fire."

Bingham's face darkened. "Seems you're assumin' a lot of authority just because you wear that badge, Gunnison. You should practice what you preach. After all, you had the gall to command me to keep my eyes off of the grieving widow over there, and then you went and kissed her up good yourself!"

Suzanne's head whipped around. Her face reddened, and she pressed her lips together in anger, glaring heatedly at Bingham. She had not been aware that he had seen their embrace the night before. She was aware that Pearl Madison was eyeing her, eyebrows raised, with a look of disapproval on her face. Suzanne wanted to shout

out loud that it was not the way it appeared, but she kept quiet and, feeling uncomfortable, looked down at her food.

Johnny Valentine's temper rose. His muscles shook with fury as he leaned on the crutches, shifting his weight to stand firmly on both feet. Staring fiercely at the gunfighter, who was still seated calmly on a nail keg three feet from him, Valentine growled, "I'm warning you, Bingham. Stay out of other people's lives. These people have had enough troubles today."

Stuart Vance wheeled and pointed an accusing finger at Bingham. "The marshal's right, Bingham. Marianna and I were doing fine until you came along and butted in! Keep away from her, or you'll be sorry."

The gunfighter rose to his feet, and his eyes flashed. "Don't threaten me, sonny," he growled. "I've *killed* men for stickin' their fingers in my face!"

Vance threw an unexpected punch at the gunfighter's jaw, knocking him down. Bingham jumped to his feet and lunged at the younger man.

The opponents went hurtling across the barn, smashing into the two barrels where the food and water were stored and knocking them over. Doreen Warrick screamed at the two men wrestling with each other, "Stop! Stop! You're destroying the supplies!"

They rolled over and over in the dirt, mashing food into the wet ground. Finally Bingham got the upper hand and got on top of the smaller man, pulling back his fist to pummel Vance's face.

Throwing down one of his crutches, Johnny Valentine limped over and grabbed Bingham's arm, yanking him off Vance and sending the gunfighter rolling. Valentine had bent to help the younger man to his feet when Bingham came charging.

"You're gonna regret that, Gunnison!"

Staggering slightly on his game leg, Valentine adjusted

his stance and met the gunfighter with a haymaker, sending Bingham down, unconscious.

"Now look what you've done, Stuart!" Marianna shouted furiously. "We're going to have to run around town again—and see all those awful dead bodies—to get more food and water."

Jason Hart hurried over and took his niece by the arm, pulling her to the far end of the barn. Everyone could hear the tone of his angry reprimand, if not the exact words. But his ward stomped imperiously away from him, saying, "I'm of age, Uncle Jason. I can do and say what I want!"

Johnny Valentine picked up his other crutch and made his way over to young Vance. Putting a fatherly arm around the young man's shoulder, he said, "Stuart, listen to some sound advice, and don't irritate Sid. He's fast with a gun, and he just might shoot first next time. He's telling the truth when he says he's killed fourteen men. Don't become number fifteen."

Stuart Vance's thin body stiffened with anger. Turning from Valentine, he hurried across the room to a pile of guns. Picking up a gun belt and a holster with a Colt .44, he strapped it on and declared, "When Bingham wakes up, he and I are gonna settle matters."

Valentine said flatly, "You can't do it, kid."

"Aw, you don't know that for certain, Marshal. I've done a little practicing at this, myself."

"He's done more than practice," warned Valentine. He glanced over at Marianna and said, "Listen, Stuart, no flirty girl is worth dying for."

"It's gone too far," snapped Vance heatedly, adjusting the gun belt.

"I'll prove you can't outdraw him," said the man with the badge. "Empty your gun. I'll do the same with mine."

The young man did as Valentine said, and then the two of them placed their guns back in their holsters.

Squaring off, Valentine said, "Now, kid, I'm not a gunfighter like Sid Bingham. If you can't outdraw me, I guarantee you won't be able to outdraw him. Now go ahead. Draw."

Vance's hand dipped for his gun. Before he could draw it from the holster, Valentine's weapon was out, cocked, and aimed at the younger man.

"Bang! You're dead!" he said loudly.

Vance's mouth gaped open, and his eyes bulged.

Reloading his gun, Valentine said calmly, "You see, son, you'd be no match for Sid Bingham. Don't challenge him. *His* gun will be loaded."

Defeat was evident on Vance's handsome young face. "But Marshal, I don't like him flirting with Marianna. It's got to stop."

"Marianna can stop it if she wants to," said the lawman.

Vance looked longingly at the pretty blonde, but she merely gave him an impudent look that said, "I don't want to."

Gritting his teeth, Vance turned away from her in disgust.

The marshal heard a groan and looked over at Sid Bingham, who was coming around. Valentine went over to help him to his feet, but Bingham shook off his hand.

"You're gonna be sorry you did that, Gunnison," he snarled.

"I'm warning you, Bingham," Valentine retorted. "It'd be in your best interest to forget it . . . and also to leave that girl alone." He turned and walked away from the gunfighter.

Suzanne Lane came over from helping Doreen to salvage some of the food. She looked up at Valentine admiringly. With concern in her voice she asked, "Are you all right, Ford? You shouldn't be on your feet so much—even though it was for a good reason." She smiled at him, and her feelings were evident.

Valentine felt his heart leap. "Yeah, I'm fine," he answered tersely, fighting off the impulse to take her in his arms and kiss her. "I just need to sit down and—"

A shutter slammed loudly shut. "Grab your weapons!" Paul Warrick shouted from his post. "The Kiowas are back!"

# Chapter Nine

After Paul Warrick's startling announcement everyone except Al Trowbridge ran to the two windows and peered out. Over thirty Kiowas, on foot and heavily armed, were moving slowly between houses and outbuildings, their nearly naked bronzed bodies gleaming in the afternoon sun.

Warrick lifted his eyes from the gun slot in the door and whipped his head around. "Close those shutters and grab a gun!" he shouted to the others, and everyone obeyed. The women ran and picked up rifles along with the men.

Johnny Valentine left his crutches where they had fallen and made his way to the door. Speaking softly, he said, "Paul, is there any other way to get into the barn besides the main door and the windows?"

"There's one other entry," Warrick responded, his eyes again peering through the gun slot in the door as he watched the Indians approaching.

"Where?"

"See that bunch of feed barrels stacked against the back wall? There's a small door behind them. It's only about four feet high and a couple of feet wide. We've got it barred with a crossbar, and those barrels are also barricading it."

Valentine looked around the barn at the others. The women stood together in the center of the big room, holding their rifles ready. The fear on their faces was visible even in the dim light. Burke Simms stood near the women, a pistol in each of his hands. When the fighting started, he would take up a position at a window, but for the moment he was speaking words of encouragement to the women. Oliver Madison and Sid Bingham were positioned at the gunports of the window farthest from the door, and Gene McKee and Jason Hart were by their sides, ready to take over when the others had to reload. Stuart Vance, a rifle in his hand, stood at the other window, waiting to be joined by Simms. Valentine and Warrick would fight alongside each other by the front door.

The Indians halted some twenty yards from the barn and spread out. A tall figure threaded his way among them to the forefront.

"Trailing-the-Enemy," Warrick said hoarsely.

Valentine peered through the slot at the renegade Kiowa chief, who was holding a shiny new Henry .44 rifle in his right hand. It was easy to see why his warriors had followed Trailing-the-Enemy, ignoring their tribal leader. The renegade chief was an awesome sight as he stood rigidly like a well-muscled, finely chiseled statue, his black hair falling onto his broad shoulders. The feathers in the Indian's long ceremonial warbonnet rippled in the breeze as he waited for just the right moment to make his move.

The chief finally raised his rifle over his head, and the two black feathers that dangled from the tip of the barrel danced in the air. Speaking loudly in a deep, guttural tone, he called out, "You in the barn! I am Trailing-the-Enemy, Kiowa chief! I would speak to your leader!"

Inside the barn, Warrick looked around and said to the others, "Who should we designate as leader?"

Dr. Simms spoke up, "I'd say that as a law enforcement officer, Marshal Gunnison is the closest thing we have to a leader in this bunch. Trailing-the-Enemy might show some respect for his badge, too."

Warrick looked at the somewhat startled impostor and nodded. "The Indian's all yours, Marshal."

Valentine ran a sweeping glance over the others, lingering briefly on the woman he loved, and then he and Warrick lifted the heavy timber crossbar from the door. He opened the door just wide enough to slip through, and then he stepped outside, cocking his revolver and pointing it to the ground.

"My name is Ford Gunnison," lied Johnny Valentine, facing the renegade Kiowa chief. "I'm a United States marshal, and I'm acting as leader here. What is it that you want?"

"Two white men ambushed three of my braves, killing two of them. The third was wounded, but he was able to return to camp with the horses. I am looking for the two white killers. Are they with you?"

Johnny Valentine was more than half sure that the two ambushers were indeed inside the barn and had lied to him. He realized now that Trowbridge and McKee had never explained how they had survived that Indian attack. But to be certain, he asked the chief, "Can you tell me what the two men looked like?"

The chief gave a detailed description of the two drifters, adding, "One of the killers was shot in the stomach."

"What will you do to these men?" Valentine asked, already suspecting the answer.

"Punish them Kiowa way," came the laconic reply.

"Let me tell my people what you have told me," Valentine said, stalling for time. He slipped back through the door and dropped the heavy crossbar into place.

His anger rising, Valentine whirled and faced the two

drifters. "You two lied to us," he hissed. "The ambush was the other way around."

McKee hurried over to Valentine and pleaded, "Don't let those savages have us, Marshal! We're sorry we did what we did, ain't we, Al?" McKee looked at his partner, then at the others. "See, we lost all our money and our horses in a card game at Larned," he explained. "We were headin' across the plains, strugglin' on foot, when we spotted them three savages comin' at us. They didn't see us 'cause we was in tall grass, and we decided to jump 'em and take two of the horses. I mean, after all, they're enemies of us whites, right? So we opened fire on 'em. That ain't so awful, now, is it?"

"Why did you give us that cock-and-bull story? Why didn't you just tell us the truth?"

"Well . . . uh . . . well, we weren't sure if you'd help us if you knew what really happened. I had to make sure you'd pick us up so's we could get to a town, and Al could get doctored up."

Trailing-the-Enemy's deep voice unexpectedly rang out. "I know by your silence that you have these two men in with you! Give me the ambushers, and the rest of you will be allowed to live!"

Even though Valentine felt disgust at what McKee and Trowbridge had done, still he could not find it in him to hand them over to the Kiowas. He looked at the others and said, "These men should be delivered to the authorities for trial."

Sid Bingham stomped over to Valentine and snapped, "Listen, Gunnison, there ain't no time to do things proper, and we ain't got a chance against that many Indians. We're all doomed if we don't give the Kiowas McKee and Trowbridge. I say let 'em have 'em! We didn't ambush the chief's braves; *they* did!"

"He's right," agreed Oliver Madison. "Why should we pay with our lives for their stupidity?"

"What you're talking about is the same as murder!" exclaimed Valentine. "These men made a grievous mistake, I grant you, but we can't turn them over knowing they'll be tortured." He looked around. "We can make a stand. This barn is as strong as a fort, and there's got to be a search party out looking for us by now. It'll probably be a matter of hours before they come to Pawnee Rock."

Jason Hart shook his head in disagreement. "What if it takes them longer than that? All the Indians have to do is surround the barn and wait. We've got practically no food and water now—thanks to the fight you and that gunfighter had, Stuart." He gave the younger man a baleful stare, and Vance blanched. "We've got them to think of," Hart added, his hand sweeping toward the women. "I say let's give the Kiowas what they want—Trowbridge and McKee."

"I agree, Marshal," Burke Simms declared.

Valentine looked at his old friend in astonishment. "Whatever happened to the Hippocratic oath, Doc? Aren't you sworn to save lives?"

"Of course I am!" the elderly physician declared. "I don't like throwing these two men to the wolves any more than you do, but on the other hand, Mr. Hart is right. We *do* have the women to consider. If we give the Indians these men, who after all did break the law—both man's law and God's law, I might add—there might be a chance for the rest of us. If we don't . . . well, I don't think we have any choice."

"I'd say you're outvoted, Marshal," Paul Warrick said. "Let's do what Trailing-the-Enemy wants."

Valentine peered narrowly at Warrick. "What makes you think those Kiowas will go away just because we give them Trowbridge and McKee?"

With a mixture of anger and fear in his voice, Paul Warrick glared at Valentine and said, "In case you don't know it, Marshal, it's a matter of pride with Indians to keep their word."

"I know a good deal about Indians," came Valentine's raspy reply. "They're not all of the same cut." Pointing at the door, Valentine said emphatically, "The very fact that he's standing there right now is proof his word doesn't mean a thing."

Warrick shook his head. "You're talking in riddles, Gunnison."

"Chief Kicking Bird, the Kiowa leader, signed a treaty with the whites ten years ago at Medicine Lodge, Kansas. Kicking Bird and all of his people agreed to settle on a reservation in the Oklahoma Indian Territory. The treaty stipulated that the entire Kiowa nation would stay on the reservation and never again make war on the whites. But since then, several renegade Kiowas have left the reservation, disregarding Kicking Bird's treaty. These renegades have raided towns and settlements in Oklahoma, Texas, and Kansas." He jerked his thumb and said, "Trailing-the-Enemy is one of those renegades."

Rubbing his chin and looking at his feet, Warrick nodded and said, "I suppose so. . . ."

"Then where's this pride you talked about? The man has broken his word."

Hoping his words were sinking in, Valentine added, "Since that chief out there broke his word about staying on the reservation, what makes you think he'll keep it now? I'm telling you—all of you—if we hand over Trowbridge and McKee, it won't be the end of it. Trailing-the-Enemy has already attacked the barn twice. He won't be satisfied until every inhabitant is dead. And that *is* a matter of pride!"

After a long silence Suzanne said quietly, "What the marshal said makes good sense. If he's right and the Kiowas do attack us, Mr. McKee could handle a gun. If worse comes to worst, so could Mr. Trowbridge. If we let the Kiowas have them, we'll have two fewer guns to fight them with."

Doreen Warrick nervously fingered the bandage that covered her injured eye and said to her husband, "Paul, I agree with Mrs. Lane. Maybe you should listen to the marshal."

"Aw, I don't buy this stuff!" broke in Sid Bingham. "It's different for Trailing-the-Enemy about jumpin' the reservation and about breakin' his word. How would any of us like to be cooped up on a reservation? I can't blame him for takin' off. But he *is* a redskin, and anybody knows redskins have got this thing in their heads about bein' honorable and keepin' their word. Warrick's right. That Indian will stick to his word about this. He wants the two scoundrels who up and shot his men from ambush, and he's got a right to 'em."

"That Indian out there isn't going to wait much longer, Gunnison!" bellowed Paul Warrick. "McKee and Trowbridge have to go!"

"I'm . . . I'm changing my mind," Simms suddenly declared. "Odds are pretty good that a search party's been sent out to find us—and since the authorities are aware of the Kiowa renegades, chances are the Army's taken charge of the search. I think the marshal's right. They'll probably pass by here shortly, and they'll drive the Kiowas away. I say we take a stand. I don't want the deaths of these two men on my conscience."

"Will the massacre of four innocent women weigh less heavily on your conscience?" Hart asked Simms pointedly.

"I'll fight to see that won't happen," the physician retorted.

Valentine took a deep breath and let it out slowly. "Well, since I was appointed leader here a few minutes ago, I'll just have to assert my authority. If the rest of you want to throw these men to the Indians, you'll have to go through me to get them."

"Then we'll go through you!" snapped Paul Warrick.

Valentine clenched his teeth. "One at a time, or all at once?"

The icy challenge sank into dead silence. Suzanne thought the glare in the marshal's eyes would have held a rabid wolf at bay.

The silence was shattered by a barrage of rifle shots, and bullets tore into the door and the shutters.

"Take your places, men!" Valentine shouted. "Let them have it!"

The stone barn reverberated with a thunderous roar as the Indian's gunfire was returned. The four women sat huddled together holding the loaded spare weapons, fear and anticipation mingled on their faces.

"Don't waste ammunition!" Valentine shouted above the din. "Only shoot when you've got a sure target!"

"Hey!" cried out Gene McKee. "I just hit one!"

"That don't surprise me none," Bingham said to the man standing behind him and sneered. "Shootin' Indians seems to be your cup of tea."

The desultory firing continued throughout the day. By the time the sun went down, six Kiowas had been hit. One of them had been able to crawl away, but the other five lay dead, sprawled in plain view. With darkness upon them, Trailing-the-Enemy led his men away from the scene, shouting, "We will be back with the rising of the sun! I will still let the rest of you live if you give me the two murderers! You cannot win otherwise!"

For his answer, Johnny Valentine sent a shot through the gunport in the direction of the retreating renegade chief's voice.

As the sound of the horses' hooves grew fainter, those

inside the barn breathed easy for the first time since the first shots had been fired that afternoon. Talk remained at a minimum as the lanterns were lit and a portion of their meager food was passed around. No one complained about the rations; they were glad to have survived the attack unscathed.

Paul Warrick looked at the marshal and said, "Well, since you've gotten your way, Gunnison, tell us what we're going to do when the food and water are gone."

"Surely the Army will find us soon," Simms said optimistically.

"I don't think we can just sit back and wait, Doc," said Valentine. "The Kiowas might get the upper hand before too long. Our best bet is for one man to slip out under cover of darkness and go to Fort Zarah for help. It's not that far—maybe fifteen or sixteen miles."

Sid Bingham snorted. "That's easy for you to suggest. With your leg in a splint, you *can't* go. Them Indians will be out there, just waitin' for us to try somethin' foolish like that. I'll tell you this much right now. *I* ain't goin' on no suicide mission."

"There's no doubt it will be risky," said the physician. "But it has to be done. Somebody's got to try, so I'll be that somebody."

Valentine quickly said, "Sorry, Doc, I can't let you try it. For one thing, your age is against you. For another, we need you here to tend any wounded."

"I still say all we have to do is give the Kiowas McKee and his pal, and that'll be the end of it," Paul Warrick said bitterly.

"You're as wrong as you can be," growled Valentine. "You can't trust Trailing-the-Enemy's word as far as you could throw this barn. But how about it, Warrick? Are you willing to make a dash for Fort Zarah?"

"Nope," he said flatly. "I agree with Sid. It would be nothing short of suicide."

Jason Hart said, "If somebody's got to try it, why not send McKee? If it weren't for him and his partner, we wouldn't be in this fix."

"I disagree!" Suzanne Lane exclaimed. "The Kiowas hit this town before you ever laid eyes on Mr. McKee and Mr. Trowbridge. They'd have come back to finish the job whether we were here or not. What will it take to convince you that the marshal is right? The chief is lying about letting the rest of us go free if he gets his two victims."

Hart had nothing to say by way of a rejoinder.

"What about you, Stuart?" Marianna Freeman asked. "You're certainly able-bodied. Are you afraid?"

Stuart reddened with anger. "Of course I'm not afraid," he snapped. "I just happen to agree with your uncle. There's no sense getting killed needlessly. Besides, you need my protection from Bingham."

Marianna merely sniffed and turned away in disgust.

Oliver Madison put his hand affectionately on his wife's shoulder. Then he stood up and said to Valentine, "I've been thinking about what you said, Marshal. You're probably right about that Indian. Giving him these men would not change a thing, most likely. Our only hope is to make sure the Army gets here soon. I'll go."

Pearl's face went pale. Standing to look her husband in the eye, she said tremulously, "Ollie, no! I won't let you leave me! Mr. Bingham is right. It would be suicide for anyone to go out there!"

"It would be suicide to sit here and do nothing about our predicament, honey," Madison retorted. "We can't guarantee when the Army'll come, and those Indians outnumber us by far too many. I'm doing this for your sake more than for anyone else's. If we don't get help, you might be tortured and killed. I can't let that happen. Please, understand—I must go."

Pearl held her husband tightly for several minutes. Then she kissed him and reluctantly released him. While Madison strapped on a gun belt and stuffed extra cartridges in his pockets, Johnny Valentine hobbled to the door and peered through one of the gun slots.

"There's pretty good cloud cover, Oliver," the impostor said. "The little moonlight'll make it harder for you to see where you're going—but harder for the Kiowas to see you, as well." He turned around and looked at the volunteer. "Lucky you're wearing a dark-colored shirt, too—and you'll put the odds even more in your favor if you crawl out on your belly."

Madison kissed Pearl one more time, telling her that he loved her. Then he stepped over to the door and said to Valentine, "I'm ready."

At Valentine's command the lanterns were put out, enveloping the inside of the barn in darkness. Paul Warrick groped his way to the door in the thick gloom and helped lift off the crossbar. Then he quietly slid the latch and opened the door carefully to keep it from squeaking. As Oliver Madison dropped to his belly, Warrick whispered, "I honestly don't think you have a chance, Madison, but good luck to you."

Madison did not answer. He began a slow crawl, inching his way along the front of the barn. He heard the door softly shut, followed by the faint metallic clank of the latch being thrown. He was on his own now.

Inside the darkened barn Suzanne Lane found her way to Pearl and put her arms around the softly sobbing woman. "He'll be fine, Pearl. Ford—Marshal Gunnison—thinks Oliver has a good chance," she said encouragingly, hoping her words did not sound as false to Pearl as they did to her.

The men decided they should take shifts on watch, allowing the others to get some sleep. Paul Warrick made his way to one of the windows and quietly opened the shutter. He would take the first watch.

Stuart Vance walked in the dark to where Marianna lay, and he knelt down beside her. Speaking in a whisper, he said, "I'm staying close to you tonight. I'll be right here if you need me."

The blonde whispered caustically, "What are you, Stuart, my watchdog?"

"Call me whatever you want, Marianna. I love you, and I care what happens to you."

"Nothing's going to happen to me. And if you're referring to Sid, it's none of your business!"

"Marianna, when are you going to realize that he cares nothing for you, except that you're female?"

"Pshaw!" she snapped. "Sid is genuinely attracted to me. I can see it in his eyes."

"What you see in his eyes is lust, Marianna, nothing more. If you were as worldly as you think you are, you would recognize it."

In a huff, Marianna Freeman rolled over and went to sleep.

Oliver Madison bellied his way past the barn and the corral, breathing a sigh of relief when he reached the deep shadows of a cluster of cottonwood trees. Peering around carefully, he rose to his feet, elated to have made it this far. Now that the Indian danger was almost behind him, he would get on the road that led to Great Bend, which was about sixteen miles away. Fort Zarah was two or three miles beyond the town. If he paced himself so as not to run out of strength, he would reach the fort by dawn. The cavalry could be at Pawnee Rock shortly after sunup—just in time to prevent another Kiowa attack.

Strong arms suddenly enfolded him, and a rough hand clamped down on his mouth, keeping him from crying out. He was quickly disarmed and dragged to a house that was out of sight of the barn. Roughly shoved into the kitchen and tied to a chair, Madison feared his pounding heart would burst. He gamely tried to keep the absolute terror he felt from showing on his face, but he knew it was useless.

The door behind him came open, and from the look on the Indians' faces he guessed who had entered. He twisted his head around, and the savage fierceness in Trailing-the-Enemy's eyes chilled Oliver Madison's blood. The Kiowa who accompanied the chief came close to Madison and stood staring down at him before placing the point of a razor-sharp knife to the captive's Adam's apple.

While the brave called Black Beaver held the knife to Madison's throat, Trailing-the-Enemy stood in front of him and demanded, "What is your name, white man?"

Madison stuttered out his name, his eyes wide with fear.

"Now, Oliver Madison, tell me the names of the two men who ambushed my braves."

With quivering lips, Oliver stammered, "Uh . . . one's n-name is . . . G-Gene McKee. Th-the other is Al Trowbridge. P-please, sir! Please, don't kill me, I beg you!"

Ignoring Madison's plea, Trailing-the-Enemy barked, "How many people are in the barn?"

Shaking as if he had just emerged from a lake of ice water, Madison blurted, "My wife is in there, sir! I'll tell you anything you want to know, but please promise me you won't hurt Pearl or any of the rest of us. We didn't do you any harm. Please!"

"You tell me what I want to know, and you and your squaw will live," the chief grunted.

The Kiowa leader listened as Oliver Madison described each person in the barn, noting those who were wounded or injured. Over the next half hour, Madison answered every question put to him: the number of firearms in the barn, how much ammunition the white men had, and how long the supply of food and water would last. The renegade chief was surprised to learn about the well-fortified small door at the back of the barn.

When Trailing-the-Enemy seemed satisfied that he had all the information he needed, he took three of the Kiowa braves into another room of the house, leaving the white man to tremble uncontrollably and wonder what was coming next.

After several long minutes the chief and his men returned to the captive, and Trailing-the-Enemy, said, "You will be released now, Oliver Madison." He then told Black Beaver to untie him.

A smile of relief broke over Madison's face. "Oh, thank you, sir!" he gasped. "Thank you! You *will* spare my wife also, won't you? And the other innocent people in the barn?"

"Of course." Trailing-the-Enemy nodded, regarding the white man with steady, obsidian eyes.

"Excuse me, sir, but how will you get the two ambushers out of the barn without harming the others? Some of those people are pretty determined that you won't get Trowbridge and McKee."

A slight smile touched the chief's lips. "Black Beaver will explain everything to you outside."

# Chapter Ten

Two hours before dawn Johnny Valentine rose from the spot where he had been sleeping on the barn floor and stretched his cramped body. He hobbled on his makeshift crutches to the window where Burke Simms was keeping watch and whispered, "My turn, Doc. See if you can get a little more sleep before daylight."

"Johnny," breathed Simms, "if Madison doesn't get through, we're doomed."

"Keep your chin up, Doc," Valentine whispered.

"I'm trying." The older man patted the impostor on the shoulder, then moved away in the dark.

Bracing himself on the crutches, Valentine peered through the unshuttered window. The moon had apparently run its arc across the heavens, and it was even darker now than it had been earlier. Clouds obscured most of the stars, and he could barely make out the buildings across the way. Not a thing was moving in Pawnee Rock that he could detect.

Valentine had been at the window almost an hour when he heard the soft rustle of skirts behind him. He knew it was Suzanne Lane even before she was close enough for him to discern her vague features in the gloom.

Touching his arm, she whispered, "How's your leg feeling?"

"Nothing unbearable," he responded. "Just a constant dull ache."

"I wish there was something I could do for you," she said.

"Your concern is more than enough."

Squeezing his arm and pressing herself close to him, Suzanne softly admitted, "Oh, Ford! I'm so terribly frightened!"

Bracing himself on one crutch, Valentine leaned the other against the wall and gently put his arm around her shoulders. He wanted to tell her how he felt about her, but he had promised himself he would not. If they lived through this desperate situation, he still had to remove himself from Suzanne's life.

Valentine's resolve weakened still further when the captivating redhead raised her face to his. He felt her warm breath on his face, and then she tenderly kissed him.

"Ford, do you think it's possible to fall in love under these circumstances—with Frank's death and everything that's happened these last few days? I keep telling myself that it just can't be possible—but my heart tells me differently."

Valentine was quiet for several moments. He knew beyond a shadow of a doubt that he had fallen in love with her as well, but he also knew that he must not allow their love to grow any deeper. Even if they lived through the Indian siege, he had no choice but to ride off and leave her—even though something vital in him would be destroyed. He would never be the same for having known Suzanne and loved her. He knew that disappearing from her life would be the easiest course of action for both of them. She would feel such an intense hatred for him when she learned the truth—and if he stayed in her life, she would inevitably find out who he really was. No, by his leaving she would be protected from that awful truth. She must never know that the man in whom she had invested her feelings was the man who had killed her husband.

"Ford?" she said again gently.

He cleared his throat. "I would be lying if I said I didn't love you," he whispered. "But I'm no good for you. If only you knew—"

She pressed her soft, cool fingers to his lips. "All I need to know is that you love me. If we truly love each other, there is nothing we can't overcome."

Overwhelmed by her love, Valentine pulled her close and kissed her passionately, feeling the fire of it course through his body. Then, just as suddenly, he released her. His throat was tight, and his heart felt as though it would burst. Of all the women in the world, why did he have to fall in love with Frank Lane's widow?

"Ford . . . ?" she said, invading his thoughts. "Is there something wrong?"

Valentine was waging a fierce battle with himself. Because he loved her, he wanted her to know the truth—then and there. This masquerade he had involved her in was tearing his heart out.

"Suzanne, I can't let you love me. Believe me, I'm no good for you, I'll only make you unhappy. I—"

His confession was cut off when Suzanne kissed him again. "Hush!" she whispered. "I don't want to hear any talk about your not being good enough for me. I know that you are a good, kind, considerate, and honest man. Whatever obstacles we might face because of your profession can be worked out. I promise."

With the joy of love filling her heart, Suzanne hugged him tightly and kissed him one more time. Then she released him. She sighed deeply as her thoughts returned to the terrible reality of their situation. "We probably should eat breakfast while it's still dark outside," she said. "Once it's light the Kiowas are sure to attack."

"You're right," Valentine said hoarsely, trying to clear his head. "I'll wake the menfolk while you wake the women."

Soon everybody in the barn was up, and by the pale light of one lantern they ate more of their rations. They talked quietly as they ate, and soon it was apparent that Oliver Madison was on everybody's mind.

"Your husband should be at Fort Zarah by now," Suzanne Lane said, stepping close to Pearl and patting her shoulder. "No doubt he and the troops will be here soon, and this horrible nightmare will be over."

Pearl looked at her and forced a smile. The worry she felt was evident in her bloodshot eyes.

Stuart Vance looked over his shoulder at the now-shuttered window, which Johnny Valentine had closed when he sat down to eat. Pulling out his pocket watch, Vance read the time and realized that outside their stone fortress, dawn had begun to break. He left Marianna's side and went to the window, cautiously pushing open the shutter a few inches. Hearing him gasp, everyone looked in his direction.

"Marshal!" choked out the young man. "Come here!"

Valentine grabbed his crutches and made his way to Vance's side. The others followed suit, crowding around the two front windows to look out. As the shutters were thrown back, the horrid scene before them stunned the whole group. Pearl Madison screamed as she jumped back in horror.

The growing light of dawn revealed the naked body of Oliver Madison hanging upside down from a limb of the cottonwood tree some fifty feet across from the front of the barn. The early morning breeze was causing the body to sway slightly, making the sight even more horrible. Madison had been stabbed dozens of times and then disemboweled, and his sightless eyes bulged from their sockets, frozen in a look of terror.

Suzanne started toward Pearl to comfort her, but the frantic, screaming woman suddenly dashed to the big door, lifted the crossbar from its place, threw the latch, and darted outside. She ran toward her husband's bloody corpse, screeching his name. Suzanne and Valentine yelled at her to come back, but she never even heard them: A staccato of rifle fire opened up from outside.

Bullets tore into Pearl's body, knocking her to the ground. She stumbled to her feet and staggered with outstretched hands toward the tree where her husband was hanging, crying, "Ollie! Ollie! Ollie!"

Another volley of shots ended her life. There were at least two dozen bullets in her as she fell beneath her husband's swaying body.

Within seconds Paul Warrick and Johnny Valentine had slammed the barn door shut, barring and locking it. The other men dashed to their fighting positions and unleashed a barrage of gunfire at the Kiowas. Two of the Indians were dropped before they could pull back to the safety of the buildings.

When the shooting stopped, Warrick turned on Valentine, his face livid with fury. With barely controlled anger he hissed, "This is your fault, Gunnison! We ought to throw you out there so you can get what Pearl and Oliver Madison got. If you had let us turn these dirty, lying drifters over to the Indians, none of this would have happened. Two innocent people are dead because of your asinine bullheadedness! I hope you can live with yourself."

Sid Bingham jumped in with both feet. "Yeah, Marshal. *You* killed that man and his wife. If you'd given Trailing-the-Enemy what he wanted, McKee and Trowbridge would be hangin' in that tree, not Oliver Madison. Pearl Madison would still be alive, and the Indians would be gone!"

The temper that Suzanne was trying to keep in check caught fire. Stomping over to the gunfighter, she said heatedly, "Just because the Kiowas killed Oliver Madison doesn't mean they would have gone away peacefully if Trowbridge and McKee had been handed over to them! You seem to be forgetting that the Kiowas raided Pawnee Rock for absolutely no reason! If I were a man, Mr. Bingham, I would make my point more forcefully. What you need is—"

Suzanne's tirade was interrupted by a hand on her shoulder. "What you need," Valentine interjected, "is to learn more about renegade Indians. Trailing-the-Enemy is a truce breaker. He is not trustworthy."

"You're basing your assumption on absolutely nothing, Gunnison," Jason Hart declared. "For all you know, Trailing-the-Enemy would have left us all in peace if we had turned Trowbridge and McKee over to them, and Oliver and Pearl Madison would still be alive!"

Again McKee and Trowbridge looked on with trepidation. It was plain that their fate lay in the hands of the man who wore the badge.

Burke Simms leaped to Valentine's defense, and then Stuart Vance cast his lot with the marshal and the doctor. "I agree with them. No one can blame Marshal Gunnison for the deaths of the Madisons. Oliver freely volunteered to go for help, fully aware of the danger."

Vance's softspoken words had somewhat of a calming effect. When they had all cooled down a bit, Valentine said, "We're wasting a lot of energy arguing. You can bet your boots that those savages are going to make every effort to come in here and kill all of us. Our chances of coming out of this situation are plenty slim—but I have an idea that might save a few of us."

Paul Warrick had the impulse to draw a gun on Gunnison and say he had an idea that would save *all* of them: Give the Kiowas the two drifters. But Warrick was not sure Hart and Bingham would back him up.

"What's your idea, Marshal?" asked Simms.

Pointing to a far corner of the barn, Valentine said, "We can dig a hole back there. Even with the door and the windows open, very little light reaches back there. We can make the hole big enough for two people, maybe three. The dirt can be covered with hay from up in the loft, so it won't be noticed. We can use a gate from one of the horse stalls to cover the hole, then camouflage the gate with more straw."

"Are you thinking that a couple of people can hide in the hole and not be found by the Indians?" asked Stuart Vance. He was looking at Marianna Freeman.

Nodding, Valentine replied, "We have no way of knowing how it's going to go, but after the last battle there might be a couple of survivors who could jump into the hole, slide the lid over it, and hide. Maybe the Kiowas will only make sure those they can see are dead and then leave. If so, whoever is in the hole will be able to tell the story of what happened here."

Doreen Warrick's face was chalk-white. "Marshal," she said, licking her lips, "you don't see any hope for us, do you?"

"I won't say I don't see *any* hope, ma'am," he said solemnly, "but we must face the fact that our chances are indeed slim. I doubt that anyone else here wants to try to run for Fort Zarah."

"You keep forgetting that we have two cards yet to play in this game, Gunnison," said Paul Warrick, a raw edge to his voice. "McKee and Trowbridge."

Valentine turned and stared at Warrick. "I will not waste any more breath on that subject," he said, and then he walked away.

Gene McKee quickly walked over to where a shovel leaned against a wall. He picked it up and walked to the far corner of the barn. Knowing that the best way to garner support was to make himself useful, he threw himself into the task at hand, and soon Burke Simms grabbed another shovel and began digging as well.

Watching the two men, Jason Hart turned to Vance and said, "Well, Stuart, let's get a gate from one of the horse stalls."

Vance glanced over at Marianna, who was standing next to Sid Bingham.

"Ever the faithful watchdog, aren't you, Vance?" the gunfighter sneered.

"Go help Uncle Jason," Marianna said sullenly. "I'd like the company of a *real* man for a change."

Johnny Valentine's voice cut across the barn, "If you don't mind, little lady, you could do us all a favor by standing watch at one of the windows. Don't open the shutter at all, just peer through the gunport. Call out immediately if you see Kiowa activity of any kind."

Marianna moved to the window after giving Valentine a cold stare.

Looking at the gunfighter, Valentine added, "And you, Bingham, you can spell Doc on that shovel periodically."

For a moment Sid Bingham looked as if he might refuse to obey, but the steely look in the lawman's eyes kept him in line

With everyone taking turns with the digging, the hole was finished and the camouflaged gate placed over it in less than an hour. They were putting the final touches to their hiding place when Marianna called from the window,

"The Kiowas are coming—and they've got two big fence-posts! Oh, dear God, they're going to ram the door!"

"Get to your places and start shooting!" bellowed Valentine. He told Suzanne, Doreen, and Marianna to arm themselves and duck behind the kegs and boxes scattered in the middle of the floor. "You ladies start shooting if the door gives way. Don't worry about taking careful aim; just keep firing at the opening."

Suzanne's eyes fell on her purse, which lay on a nearby box. The loaded .38 was still inside. She started for it, then grabbed a rifle instead, deciding it would be a more effective weapon.

Al Trowbridge leaned against his box, a cocked .45 in his hand. He had come this far without falling into the hands of the Kiowas; he was not about to give up without a fight.

Trailing-the-Enemy must have signaled his braves to return the group's gunfire, for the Kiowa guns thundered, chewing up the shutters with a hailstorm of lead and providing cover for the other Kiowas who were charging the barn door with both battering rams.

The rapid fire kept the whites from clearly drawing a bead on the Indians, and they had to pull back from the windows repeatedly to keep from being hit. Valentine finally got off a shot that hit its mark—the lead brave carrying one of the posts. This slowed the men behind him only briefly before another brave took the place of the one Valentine had shot. The other team, however, hit the door with all their might, and the impact made a roar like a cannon, shaking the heavy wooden doorframe.

Ignoring Valentine's directive to keep down, Suzanne stayed where she was and stood with her rifle held ready, squarely facing the door. Near her, Doreen struggled to maintain her composure. She bit down hard on her lips while switching hands on the rifle so she could wipe her sweaty palms on her soiled dress.

Marianna Freeman, however, stood behind Suzanne trembling like a leaf in the autumn wind, whimpering in terror as she gripped the rifle in her hands, totally incapable of using it. Each time the huge posts bashed the door, her body jerked. Instinctively trying to distance herself from the terrifying scene, she mindlessly started backing away from the others, her eyes fixed on the big door. After several minutes she was within a few feet of the back wall.

The gallant men defending the barn door fought on, but they knew with each savage blow from the battering rams that it was going to break and shatter at any time. There were already holes in it that had splintered off, letting in more daylight.

Jason Hart leaned close to his gunport and was ready to fire when a slug whistled through the slot into the barn. He howled and stepped back, putting his fingertips to his cheek. It was barely bleeding, but it felt as though a red-hot iron had been laid next to the skin.

Over the thunder of the two battering rams echoing through the barn and the earsplitting gunfire from both sides, no one heard the pounding at the small door at the rear of the stone structure, generated by another group of Kiowas. Within minutes the door gave way, and three Kiowas filed into the barn, quickly pushing aside the barricade of feed barrels.

The first one through the opening looked at the blond woman standing directly in front of him, her back to him, totally unaware of his presence. With a fiendish grin on his face the renegade seized Marianna from behind, clamping a hand over her mouth. The strong warrior dragged her toward the small door as she kicked and clawed for her life.

Then some unexplainable sixth sense caused Suzanne

Lane to look over her shoulder. When she saw what was happening to Marianna, she gasped, and before she had time to react, the second Kiowa brave had climbed through the small door. Instantly he started toward Suzanne, but when he was only ten feet from her, she whirled and fired at him like a veteran Indian fighter. The .44 slug tore into the Kiowa's stomach, dropping him.

By then the third Indian was already through the back door, and from the set of his eyes, Suzanne could see that he was planning to head for Doreen. Stunned for a moment from what had just taken place, she stared in a daze at the bronze-skinned man, but then, realizing that Doreen was also frozen with fear, she worked the lever of her rifle, took quick aim, and downed the Kiowa. He fell several yards short of Doreen's feet.

Suzanne began to look around for Marianna, but her attention was quickly drawn to another Kiowa climbing in through the small back door. This time when she levered her rifle, it jammed momentarily, giving the Indian time to get in and run toward her. The Kiowa, who also carried a rifle, made a lunge for Suzanne as she was finally levering the cartridge into her weapon's chamber. She side-stepped him, and he sailed past her, heading for the floor.

Shouting at the top of her lungs, Suzanne called for help. At that instant she saw yet another Kiowa slipping through the back door. Bringing her gun to bear, she shot him square in the chest. The bullet exploded his heart, and he died on his feet.

Somehow amid the earsplitting racket Suzanne's voice had carried to the front of the barn, and Johnny Valentine heard her call. Ignoring his throbbing leg, he made a frantic dash toward her, pausing long enough to hurl his empty revolver as hard as he could at the Indian who had fallen near Suzanne.

The fallen Indian winced as Valentine's revolver struck

him on the bridge of the nose, staggering him momentarily. Valentine closed in, wrenching the rifle from the Indian's hands, but then his game leg gave out on him, causing him to stumble and drop the rifle. It gave the Indian time to shake the fog from his head and pull a long-bladed knife from the sheath at his waist. When the half-naked warrior saw that his opponent had lost his footing, he took advantage of the moment by leaping on Valentine, wrestling him to the ground. Valentine struggled to stay clear of the deadly blade.

Seeing the danger that Valentine was in, Suzanne shouldered her rifle, attempting to get a clear shot at the Kiowa, but it was impossible. The two thrashing men were changing positions too fast. Then a shot was fired from behind her, and she turned, bringing her rifle to bear.

Al Trowbridge was balancing on his side, his smoking revolver in his hands. Another Kiowa lay dead just inside the small door. "They can only come through there one at a time!" he shouted to Suzanne, gesturing at the opening. "I'll cover it! You keep trying to help the marshal!"

Suzanne nodded and whirled around again, determined to help the man she loved. The Indian was gritting his teeth, trying to free his knife hand, but his opponent's grip was unbreakable.

But when more Indians began forcing their way through the small door, Trowbridge shouted for help, and Suzanne and Paul Warrick joined the fight, firing repeatedly at the intruders.

Doreen Warrick started to run for cover, but then she stood her ground, realizing she was needed more where she was. Raising her rifle hesitantly, she aimed at the rear door.

Suddenly there was an enormous crash, and the big front door swung open as both battering rams hit it at the same time. Sid Bingham and Stuart Vance stood shoulder to shoulder with guns blazing as the renegade Indians came pouring in, whooping and howling like wolves. Burke Simms cut loose with the revolver in his hand, and Gene McKee blasted away with his shotgun, trying to stave off what seemed to be inevitable. The rest turned their weapons toward the front door—except for Al Trowbridge, who was successfully guarding the small rear entrance.

When the Indians began dropping from the thundering guns of the whites, the Kiowas started pulling back and running away from the deadly, blazing weapons, heading for shelter. They were stunned at the fighting prowess of the people in the barn, with women fighting like men and the normally mild townsmen facing them like trained soldiers.

The break in the battle gave the defenders time to catch their breath. Simms and Hart ran to the big barn doors and pulled them closed again. The doors were practically off their hinges, but there was no point in giving the Kiowas more of an advantage than they already had.

Suzanne wheeled about to see where Valentine was and caught her breath.

The marshal had finally wrenched the knife from the Kiowa's hand. Straddling his enemy, Valentine raised the weapon and plunged it into the Indian's heart. He saw the knowledge of death in the Indian's eyes, and a moment later the man lay still, staring unseeing at the victor's face over him.

Bingham and Hart hurried over to each of the Indians who had fallen under the defenders' bullets, checking to make certain they were all dead.

Johnny Valentine let out his breath and eased himself away from the dead Kiowa, but his knees suddenly buckled, and Suzanne rushed up to him and supported him.

"Oh, Ford!" she exclaimed, taking his arm. "Are you all right?"

"Just my leg," he grunted through clenched teeth. "I've got . . . got to sit down."

Suzanne was about to call for Dr. Simms to help when she saw that he was already heading toward them. Simms helped ease his old friend to the ground and began removing the cloth that held the splints on Valentine's leg.

As Simms and Suzanne tended Valentine, the other men heaved the bodies of dead Indians out the small rear door—all except Stuart Vance, who had suddenly realized he had not seen Marianna. He looked around for her, frantically calling her name.

Concerned for his niece, Jason Hart ran over to the ladder leading to the hayloft and climbed up. "Marianna!" he shouted. "Come out! It's safe now! I promise those Kiowas won't harm you!" There was no response.

Suzanne stood up, putting a clenched fist to her mouth. "Oh, dear God," she said, her voice barely more than a whisper. "One of the Indians must have taken Marianna out the back door!"

In a near panic Stuart Vance grabbed fresh ammunition and loaded his revolver. Snapping the weapon shut, he said to Jason Hart, "I'm going after her."

Hart's face was suddenly drawn and ashen. "Stuart," he said glumly, "there are too many Indians out there. You won't have a chance."

Suzanne stepped up to the young man and and touched his arm. "Mr. Hart is right," she said. "They'll kill you, Stuart."

Vance shouted, his voice filled with terror, "I can't leave her out there! You know what those beasts will do to her! I've got to go after her!"

The handsome young man strode toward the front doors. Then he stopped and confronted Sid Bingham. "You think so much of Marianna, Bingham—you want to come with me?"

Bingham shook his head. "Man's a fool to walk into a deathtrap. She don't mean nothin' to me."

"That's what I tried to tell her," Vance breathed hotly, and then he surprised the gunfighter with a solid punch to the mouth.

Not bothering to watch as Bingham went down, Vance bolted out the big door.

# Chapter Eleven

Stepping over Kiowa corpses, Stuart Vance dashed across the dusty road fronting the stone barn, averting his eyes as he hurried past the bodies of Oliver and Pearl Madison. Pausing momentarily behind the big cottonwood from which Oliver hung, Vance looked around. The only Indians he could see were the dead ones in front of the barn. The assault had cost the Kiowas dearly, but he knew that Trailing-the-Enemy would not give up. More than ever, the renegade chief would want to find a way to kill the rest of the people inside the barn.

Vance stealthily made his way along the side of the Warrick house, stopping at the front porch and surveying what he could see of Pawnee Rock. A few Kiowas were milling about, waiting for their leader's orders. In the yard of one house farther up the street, three renegades were checking their rifles. The Kiowas were licking their wounds for the moment—but only for the moment. The stillness would not last long.

Vance's attention was drawn back to the barn. He could hear hammers pounding as the men worked on the doors, attempting to repair and fortify them for the inevitable forthcoming attack.

The youth's mind was racing as he looked back up the street. The Indians had taken over many of the houses, and Marianna was probably being held captive in one of them. But which one? Somehow he had to work his way through the town without being spotted. He had to find Marianna before—

Suddenly he heard Marianna scream. He looked about, trying to determine whence the bloodcurdling sound had come. She screamed again, and the scream was followed by ribald laughter. Vance was quite sure the sounds came from a house not more than twenty yards away. Taking a deep breath, his pulse thudding in his veins, he worked his way along the backs of the houses until he reached his destination.

He drew up beside the house and flattened himself against the side wall. The windows were open, and he could hear the Indians laughing coarsely while Marianna begged and screamed. Vance could feel his fury rising in him like the tide. Rounding the corner with his rifle ready for action, he quickly drew back at the sight of a lone Kiowa standing on the porch, grinning as he watched through the parlor door with amusement.

Taking a deep breath and setting his teeth, Stuart gripped the rifle tightly and ran up behind the Kiowa. The man turned at the sound of footsteps, but it was too late. The youth brought the butt of the rifle down violently, crushing the Indian's skull, and almost without stopping he bowled through the door.

Marianna was lying on a couch with one Indian bending over her, pinning her down, while two others stood nearby. Her dress had been ripped, and the man bending over her had his hand on her exposed shoulder. Before the startled Indian could react, Vance fired his rifle. The Kiowa stiffened, then fell dead on top of Marianna. She screamed and pushed the body to the floor.

The other two Kiowas pivoted instantly and came toward Vance. With no time to lever in another cartridge, the young man threw the rifle at one of them, striking him in the face. Vance then whipped out his revolver and shot the other Indian. The remaining warrior, still staggering from the impact of the rifle hitting him, was an easy target for Stuart's revolver.

Marianna gasped Stuart's name, and he turned toward her. At the same instant an Indian ran past the window, heading for the porch. Vance thumbed back the hammer of his revolver and waited for him to appear at the door. The gun boomed, and another Kiowa was dead.

Vance knew the gunfire would draw other Kiowas in a hurry. He looked down at Marianna, who was lying there and crying hysterically, unable to move. He bent down and helped her up from the couch, noticing the welts and scratches on her bare shoulders. "Marianna, we've got to hurry!" he said.

But Marianna's knees buckled under her, and Vance realized that she was unable to make it on her own. Holding the revolver in his right hand, he lifted her into his arms and plunged out the door. He bounded off the porch and began retracing the route he had taken moments earlier, this time throwing stealth and caution to the wind.

As he ran, the young man saw more Indians emerge from nearby houses and run toward him. Every muscle in his body was strained, and he had to stay alert to the dangers all around them. One Kiowa suddenly jumped out in front of them and raised his rifle to fire. The rifle boomed but Vance zigzagged, and the bullet whirred harmlessly past the young man's head. Firing his revolver, Vance put a slug in the Kiowa's chest, killing him instantly.

Guns barked and bullets whined all around them, some

stirring up puffs of dust as they struck the ground. Vance was running through the Warrick yard when he felt something red-hot sear him in the left shoulder. He staggered slightly but kept going, holding Marianna tightly in his arms. More bullets buzzed around the young pair as they rounded the corner, and then the roof of the big stone barn was finally in sight.

Vance's heart seemed to ignite, and his lungs caught fire as he expended all of his strength in a last-ditch effort to carry Marianna to safety. "Open the door!" he screamed at the faces visible in the barn's windows. "Open the door!"

Two more Kiowa bullets suddenly tore into Vance's back, but he ignored the pain since the barn was just ahead now, and he could see Marshal Ford Gunnison standing in front of the big door with a blazing gun in each hand. He heard two Indians just behind him howl in pain as the marshal's bullets took their toll.

Vance briefly looked at the blond woman in his arms, but she had apparently fainted. "Hang on, Marianna," he panted. "Just a little farther." The young man coughed, spraying blood on Marianna's dress. A bullet nicked his left ear, and then one struck him in the right leg. He stumbled and almost fell, but he pressed on, reaching somewhere deep within for another few ounces of strength.

Everyone in the barn was shouting encouragement to the courageous young man. Safety was only a few steps away now. Finally he staggered through the door, dropped to his knees, and gently laid Marianna down. As he did so, Burke Simms noticed the two blood-soaked holes in the front of the young woman's dress.

Johnny Valentine emptied his guns at the Indians, dropping two more as he backed into the barn, yelling for someone to close the door.

Jason Hart responded to the call, and when everyone was inside and the door bolted, he ran from the doorway

and dropped to his knees by his niece's side. Taking
Marianna's hand, he looked tenderly at her. Her eyes
were fluttering, and her breathing was shallow. Hart's
eyes met the doctor's eyes and silently asked his question.

Dr. Simms sadly shook his head. He could tell that the
young woman was mortally wounded. Two Kiowa rifle
bullets had passed through Stuart Vance's slender body
and ripped into Marianna, lodging in her chest, close to
her heart. She had only minutes to live.

Simms then did a quick examination of the gallant young
man's wounds, and his sadness deepened. Blood was running in a steady stream from Vance's mouth. He would
also die very shortly.

Looking over at Marianna and then at the physician, the
young man asked weakly, "Doc . . . is she all right?"

The kindly Simms smiled reassuringly. "She's just fine,
son," he said, his voice catching. "You saved her life.
You're a real hero."

Stuart Vance smiled and collapsed.

At the sound of his voice, Marianna roused herself.
With blood seeping from her wounds, oblivious to everything else, she managed to crawl to her rescuer's side. She
put her hand on his cheek and kissed him, whispering,
"Oh, Stuart, you . . . came for me! I do love you, Stuart! I
. . . love you!"

"I . . . I love you, Marianna," gasped the dying man,
lifting a trembling hand and placing it at the back of her
neck. He smiled, and the weight of his hand fell against
her neck as he breathed out his last breath.

Marianna's head dropped on his pulseless chest.
"Stuart . . ." she mumbled. Then she, too, was still.

Dr. Simms laid his fingers alongside Marianna's neck
and said somberly, "She's gone."

Softly, Suzanne Lane began to cry. Johnny Valentine
came up beside her and put his arm around her, drawing

her close. The redhead quickly brought her emotions under control and, wiping the tears away, said to Valentine, "I'm all right, Ford. But come, you should sit down. You need to rest your leg."

Looking at the empty guns in his holsters, he replied, "What I need to do is reload. Those renegades may come back any minute."

They heard the double click of a revolver being cocked, and Suzanne and Valentine turned. Paul Warrick was holding a gun on them. "It won't be necessary to load them, Marshal," Warrick said stiffly. "Neither you nor Mrs. Lane will be using firearms here again."

Sid Bingham and Jason Hart both pulled their revolvers and came over to stand beside Warrick.

"We've been talking," Warrick continued. "When those Indians come back, we're giving them what they want."

Standing at the rear of the barn, Gene McKee looked down at Al Trowbridge. Warrick's words made his scalp prickle.

Sid Bingham turned and pointed his weapon at McKee. "Bring me your gun, McKee," he barked. "Your pal's, too!"

Sullenly McKee obeyed. As he reached the group his face was devoid of color. "Warrick," he pleaded, "you can't do this! They'll torture us! We'll end up in a tree like Oliver Madison!"

"You two should have thought of that before you ambushed the Kiowas. We didn't have anything to do with that, and I think Trailing-the-Enemy will still bargain with us. He's lost a lot of men trying to get his hands on you. I don't think he wants to lose any more. As soon as those redskins show up again, we're making a trade. Our lives for yours!"

Burke Simms looked sadly at Warrick and said, "I think you're making a big mistake, Mr. Warrick. That renegade will kill all of us if you play into his hand."

"Shut up, Doc," rasped Warrick. "I know what I'm doing."

Shrugging his shoulders, the physician then said, "Well, until the time comes when you turn these two men over to the Indians, I have an obligation to see to my patient. Excuse me."

Without waiting for a response, Simms wheeled, picked up his black bag, and moved to the rear of the barn.

Looking back at Valentine, Warrick said, "You can give me those .45s now, Marshal. And you and the lady move over there and sit down. McKee, you too."

Valentine and Suzanne sat down beside each other on a couple of kegs. Suzanne looked fearfully at Valentine, and he tried to give her a comforting look, but he was not sure that it took.

Sid Bingham holstered his gun and moved to one of the windows. "I'll keep watch for them Indians," he said to Jason Hart. "You keep an eye on the marshal."

Hart kept his gun trained on Johnny Valentine. If the marshal made a move toward the pile of rifles and handguns ten feet away, Hart would have to shoot him.

Warrick dragged the bodies of Marianna Freeman and Stuart Vance into a corner and covered them with blankets. Doreen stayed at her husband's heels, looking sadly at Suzanne.

Valentine took hold of Suzanne's hand and whispered, "Hold on. I'll think of something."

Burke Simms was trying to figure out how to reverse the situation while he put a fresh bandage on Al Trowbridge's wound. As he was finishing, Simms noticed a rifle partially buried in the straw by the back door. Apparently it had been dropped by one of the Indians who had come through that way, and Warrick, Bingham, and Hart had all overlooked it.

The elderly physician threw a furtive glance toward the

front of the barn. Jason Hart was standing watch over Valentine, Suzanne, and McKee, gun in hand. Paul Warrick and his wife were near the door, talking quietly to each other, and Sid Bingham was peering out the window.

Keeping an eye on them, the physician picked up the rifle. Trowbridge watched him with raised eyebrows. From the side of his mouth Simms whispered, "Cough!"

Trowbridge understood. Simms needed to work the lever of the gun to be sure there was a bullet in the chamber. Though it hurt his wound to do so, the drifter went into a forced spasm of coughing. Some eyes turned toward them, but from what they could see, the doctor appeared to be working on Trowbridge.

With the coughing camouflaging the noise, Simms levered a cartridge into the chamber. A live cartridge jumped out, but at least Simms knew the gun was loaded. Standing up, his heart pounding, he walked toward the front of the barn, holding the rifle parallel with his body to make it inconspicuous. No one was paying any attention to him.

Quickly bringing the rifle to bear, the aging physician barked, "Drop your gun, Hart!"

Hart's head whipped around to see the muzzle of the rifle staring at him like a single menacing eye. The Warricks looked at the physician with surprise, and Sid Bingham spun around, glaring at Simms. The gunfighter's revolver was holstered.

Johnny Valentine hurriedly stood up, fearing for his old friend. He felt Suzanne's anguish as well.

When Hart held tight to the gun in his right hand that was pointing toward the floor, Simms's face flushed, and through his teeth he blared, "I said drop it, Hart!"

"You won't shoot me, Simms!" Hart retorted.

"What makes you think so?"

"You're a man of principle. You took an oath to preserve life, not to take it."

The physician's mouth narrowed into a determined line. His voice was steely as he said crisply, "I *will* preserve lives if I stop you and these others from making a useless bargain with the Kiowas. And if I have to take yours to preserve the others, I'll do it, Hart. Don't make me prove it."

A deathly stillness settled over the interior of the big stone barn until it became almost a tangible thing. Johnny Valentine wished his leg was not in a splint. He knew he was not able to move fast if speed was necessary, but he was ready to do whatever he could.

The doctor's eyes were fastened on Hart's gun hand, unaware that at the window behind Hart, Sid Bingham's right hand was slowly dropping toward the butt of his holstered gun.

Simms grew angry at Hart's delay, and shaking the rifle in his hands, he bawled, "Drop it, Hart! Right now! Or you're a dead man!"

Sid Bingham's hand snaked down, drew the weapon, and fired. Jason Hart jumped involuntarily, expecting to feel Simms's bullet rip into him. Instead, the elderly physician buckled and fell with a breathy gasp. Dr. Burke Simms was dead.

The sun was starting to set when Sid Bingham, looking through the window, saw a few Kiowas peering at the barn from behind the house across the street. He craned his neck and saw several others watching from various vantage points. There was no sign of Trailing-the-Enemy.

Calling to Warrick, Bingham said, "Looks like the Indians are settling in to keep an eye on the barn during the night. No doubt there are others watching the back door as well."

Warrick hurried to the window and looked for himself. While he was scanning the area, Bingham asked, "Listen, why not parley right now? Put a white flag on a stick and go out there. Let's get this done with."

Turning from the window, Warrick faced Bingham. "I want this to end as much as you do—even more, probably, since I've got my wife to think of. But there's no sense asking for trouble. No, I'll wait until Trailing-the-Enemy shows himself. When he does, I'll speak to him from the door."

Johnny Valentine grabbed his makeshift crutches and hobbled over to Warrick. As he walked by Sid Bingham, Valentine glared hotly at the gunfighter, vowing to himself that Bingham would pay for killing Doc Simms. The gunfighter read Valentine's eyes and looked away uneasily.

Warrick surprised Valentine by apologizing to him. "I hope you understand that I had no choice but to disarm you, Marshal. I simply must try to save my wife while there is still time."

"I know you believe you can reason with those renegades, Warrick, but I'm asking you—*begging* you—one last time to reconsider. Mark my words, Trailing-the-Enemy will kill all of us in spite of your generosity in handing over Trowbridge and McKee. Isn't there any way I can convince you?"

"Sorry, Marshal. Even if it's the slimmest chance in the world, I've still got to take it. For Doreen's sake. Don't you care about Mrs. Lane's safety?"

"Of course I do!" Valentine exploded. "That's why I'm pleading with you to reconsider! The Army's bound to be here soon. We just have to hang on and not hand these men—and ourselves—over to be slaughtered!"

Warrick shook his head. "I trust the chief's word."

Valentine swore and angrily walked away.

Night fell, and the lanterns were lit. Suzanne and Doreen fixed a meager meal from the fast-dwindling supply of food. No words were exchanged between them, and the silence was chilling. Finally Doreen cleared her throat. Unable to meet Suzanne's gaze, she looked down and said softly, "Suzanne, I'm sorry, but it would do me no good to go against my husband's wishes."

The redhead sighed. "I understand," she replied with resignation.

Trowbridge and McKee huddled together in fear while they listened to Warrick, Bingham, and Hart discuss how they would guard their prisoners in shifts through the night. Hart would take the first shift.

During the night, while most of the others were sleeping, Valentine and Suzanne talked in low tones, not wanting their words to be overheard.

"Suzanne, those Kiowas intend to kill all of us. When Warrick goes out to talk to Trailing-the-Enemy in the morning, I'm going to put you down in the hole and slide the gate over you. When the Kiowas come in for the rest of us, I'll run out the back door and make my way to the corral, grab one of their horses, and try to lure the Kiowas away. I'll leave the door swinging, so they'll think you got away, too. I want you to promise me you'll stay in the hole until all is quiet. Understand?"

"But your bad leg! How can you possibly run fast enough?"

"Well, I've thought about that," Valentine assured her. "I figure that while the negotiation is going on—that is, until the Kiowas feel they've lulled Warrick into believing them—everyone will be so busy watching Warrick and Trailing-the-Enemy that I doubt they'll be watching the back. And the corral is close enough for me to get to pretty easily. I can get a head start."

"Oh, Ford!" she whispered. "I'm so frightened." She gripped his arm fiercely.

Lifting her chin, he looked deep into her eyes and

kissed her passionately. Then he wrapped his arms around her and held her tight. He would not tell her that he felt he had no chance of escaping the Kiowas—that he hoped only to lead them into thinking that Suzanne had escaped so they would not search the barn for her.

"Ford . . . ?"

"Yes?"

"If we somehow do get out of this fix, will . . . will you want me?"

Knowing the odds of their both surviving were tremendous, Johnny Valentine decided to ignore the barricades that would be placed between them if they tried to make a life together. Why not let Suzanne remember him fondly, holding on to the dream of what they could have had? "Yes, darling," he whispered. "I want you more than anything in this world. I want you to be my wife."

After a few moments she whispered, "Ford, I like the sound of it."

"What?"

"Suzanne Gunnison."

Valentine was glad it was too dark for her to see his expression. He kissed her again, and they cuddled close.

After a short while he could tell by her regular breathing that she was asleep. He fought off sleep for as long as he could, knowing this night together would probably be their last. But exhaustion finally won out, and he, too, fell asleep.

# Chapter Twelve

**M**orning came with the sun shining brightly. While Jason Hart and Sid Bingham took their positions at the windows, Paul Warrick stood at the big door, waiting for Trailing-the-Enemy to appear.

Johnny Valentine and Suzanne Lane sat on two kegs, trying to make the most of these last minutes together. Suzanne's purse was in her lap, and she constantly fiddled with the purse strings, tying and untying a knot in them. Valentine took hold of her shaking hands and held them tightly in his.

A weeping Gene McKee got on his knees in front of Paul Warrick. "I'm begging you, Mr. Warrick. Please, reconsider. . . . Don't let the Indians take me and Al."

Warrick shifted uncomfortably and was about to speak when Bingham shouted, "Here they come!"

Turning, Warrick looked through one of the gunports, and what he saw made his blood run cold. Some of the Kiowas were bearing lighted torches; others were carrying cans of kerosene. Leading the procession and wearing his warbonnet was Trailing-the-Enemy. Warrick quickly realized that the Indians were planning to douse the doors and shutters with the kerosene and set them on fire.

As the Indians came closer, Warrick opened the door slightly and called out, "I must speak with you, Chief Trailing-the-Enemy!"

"Step outside where I can see you," was the reply.

Doreen ran up to her husband and grabbed his arm. "Paul," she cried. "Don't go out there! Talk to them from in here."

"Don't worry, honey," he said calmly. "They want to negotiate."

Under the watchful gaze of everyone in the barn, Warrick stepped outside into the bright sunlight. Trailing-the-Enemy stepped forward, holding his rifle with both hands.

"Talk, White Eyes. I will listen."

"Do I have your word that if we give you the two men who ambushed your braves, the rest of us can go free?"

"You have my word," said the renegade chief, nodding somberly.

"Then we agree to your terms. I will get the ambushers," Warrick said, and he moved back through the doorway. Turning to the others, he declared, "I've got the chief's promise to let the rest of us live if we give them McKee and Trowbridge. Bingham, you and Hart bring them out."

Valentine confronted Warrick one last time. "I'm warning you, you're being lied to. That renegade has no intention of keeping his word."

Warrick repeated his order to Bingham and Hart to bring the drifters outside, ignoring Valentine, who sadly watched as Trowbridge and McKee were forced toward the door at gunpoint. Then Warrick turned to his wife and said, "Doreen, you come with us. If we all go out, we'll convince the chief of our sincerity."

Obediently Doreen walked next to him.

"If the Indians see these guns in our hands, won't they misunderstand?" Jason Hart asked.

"Well . . . as soon as we step outside, we'll throw our guns on the ground as a gesture of peace," Warrick suggested. "Gunnison, you and Mrs. Lane follow us."

As the others prepared to walk out the door, Valentine whispered to Suzanne, "Now's the time! Head for the hole!"

Valentine hurried over to the barrel where Hart had stashed his gun. Sliding the revolver in his belt, he quickly stuffed some .45-caliber bullets in his pockets. Then he grabbed a .44 and a small box of ammunition for it.

As the terrified redhead was slipping down into the hole, Valentine handed her the extra gun and the box of bullets. "Remember," he cautioned her, "don't come out till the coast is clear!"

Tears were brimming in Suzanne's green eyes as she looked up at him, knowing this was their farewell. With quivering lips she said, "I love you, my darling."

"I love you, too."

Valentine shoved the straw-covered gate over the hole and started heading for the back door. Rifle shots suddenly rang out, followed by screams and wails, then more shots. Looking over his shoulder out the wide-open front door, his heart sank when he saw what he had feared: Paul and Doreen Warrick and Jason Hart had been shot down.

From the corner of his eye Valentine saw Sid Bingham reenter the barn. The marshal flattened himself along a shadowed recess of the barn wall, not wanting to be seen. He watched as Bingham darted through the shadows of the barn and out the back door, leaving the small door open and swinging in the breeze. Apparently Bingham had not been fired upon at the same time as the Warricks and Hart, and that momentary delay had given him the few seconds he needed to dive back into the barn. Valentine knew the Kiowas would run through the door at any moment, looking for Bingham as well as Suzanne and himself.

Suddenly Valentine realized that Bingham had unwittingly taken the role of decoy, which Valentine had expected to play in order to keep the Indians away from Suzanne. Valentine's best chance now was to hide in the hole with her.

Kneeling down, he placed his fingers under the edge of the gate and whispered, "Suzanne, it's me! Don't shoot!" Hurriedly he dropped into the hole and slid the hay-covered lid back in place.

"Ford, what happened?" she gasped.

In the darkness of their hiding place he found Suzanne's hands and gripped them. "I tried to warn them!" he whispered, directly into her ear. "As soon as McKee and Trowbridge were handed over to the Kiowas, the Warricks and Jason Hart were shot down."

"Oh, no!" she gasped, then whispered back, "What about Bingham?"

Valentine, appreciating the irony of the gunfighter's inadvertent help, told Suzanne what had happened. "Let's hope that the Kiowas will think that all three of us slipped away together. They'll probably catch up with Bingham before too long, but with luck they'll think that we each ran in a separate direction and will figure the two of us escaped."

Suzanne squeezed his fingers. "Oh, Ford! Maybe we still have a chance!"

A cold hand seemed to clamp down on Johnny Valentine's spine, and he had never felt more torn. He and Suzanne *did* have a chance. Maybe they *would* make it! But if they did, he would hurt this sweet, wonderful woman beyond imagination. He had meant what he had said about wanting her for his wife, but he would never have told her his feelings if their situation had not seemed so hopeless. A wave of nausea ran through his body as he realized what would happen if they did live: As soon as she was safe, he would have to disappear from her life without a word.

Suddenly the air was filled with the screams of Trowbridge and McKee.

"They'll torture them unmercifully now," Valentine whispered sadly. Putting his arms around Suzanne, they huddled together silently in the dark pit.


Outside, Al Trowbridge and Gene McKee were tied naked to the trunk of the same cottonwood tree where Oliver Madison's fly-covered body still hung. As though to make their ordeal more difficult to endure, the Kiowas had tied the two men in such a way that they had a clear view of the bullet-riddled bodies of Paul and Doreen Warrick and Jason Hart, which lay in pools of blood. The heartless renegades had poured kerosene on the two drifters' feet and then ignited it, and the two men were screaming their throats raw while the horrid smell of burnt flesh filled the air.

Trailing-the-Enemy and his warriors stood laughing, enjoying the agony of the ambushers. As the fires began to burn out, the chief instructed his men to pour kerosene a little higher on the two men's legs and ignite them again. Turning from the spectacle, the renegade chief looked around for one of his underlings. Calling him over, he asked, "Young Hawk, where have you put the others from the barn?"

Young Hawk stepped close. "We looked in through the door, and the ones inside the barn were all dead—the young woman we had captured, the one who rescued her, and the old man the white eyes said was a doctor."

Trailing-the-Enemy's eyes narrowed angrily. "There are three others besides!" the chief said furiously.

Young Hawk's features paled. "I am sorry, Chief. I did not count properly. I will go back and search thoroughly now."

"Make haste!" the Kiowa leader bellowed. "We must not allow any of them to get away!" He watched intently as Young Hawk and four other warriors ran into the barn, and then his attention was drawn back to the two men being sadistically tortured.

McKee and Trowbridge screamed for mercy. Instead, the vengeful chief ordered his men to pour kerosene still higher on their bodies and light it.

Young Hawk and his four men ran inside the barn, and as soon as they saw the back door swinging in the breeze, they knew the three white people had escaped. To be certain, they searched every part of the structure but found no one, as they had expected.

Suzanne Lane and Johnny Valentine waited breathlessly down in the dark hole, guns ready. They could hear the Kiowas running about and speaking to each other, but neither of them could understand a word of the Kiowa language. From the tone of their voices, however, they knew the Indians were furious.

Suzanne laid a trembling hand on Valentine's arm when a fresh round of screams filled the air. Whatever it was the Kiowas were doing, they were making McKee and Trowbridge die horribly and slowly. The two survivors wondered whether Sid Bingham had managed somehow to outwit the renegades, or whether his screams would soon be joining the others.

Young Hawk returned with his men to Trailing-the-Enemy and, expecting to bear his leader's wrath, hesitated a moment before speaking. "There is no one else in the barn. The three other whites have escaped."

"Escaped!" roared Trailing-the-Enemy. "How is that possible? Are you sure you searched thoroughly?"

"Yes, my chief."

"Then they cannot have gotten far! Find them!"

"Yes, at once!" responded Young Hawk, and he wheeled away.

The chief looked back at the two drifters, his fury rising. From their chests down, their bodies were blackened, and little curls of smoke were rising from the horribly burned skin. Trailing-the-Enemy could see that the men were all but dead. With a note of disgust in his voice the chief said to his warriors, "White men are weak. Very weak. They die easy. Go ahead. Use the rest of the kerosene."

The strong-smelling fluid was poured over the drifters' heads, running through their hair and dripping into their gaping mouths. Barely conscious, the two men sputtered. Trailing-the-Enemy gave the command, and matches were struck against tinderboxes one last time. The tiny flames licked at the fuel, and McKee and Trowbridge instantly became human torches. They finally, mercifully, died, screaming at the top of their lungs.

Trailing-the-Enemy left the smoldering corpses of the two drifters and returned to the Pawnee Rock house that he had been using as his headquarters. He waited impatiently for almost an hour before Young Hawk returned from his search. When Young Hawk finally arrived and slid from the back of his horse, Trailing-the-Enemy was sitting on the porch, fanning away the hordes of flies that were attracted to all the corpses strewn around the town.

The Kiowa chief stood up and crossed his arms. "I do not see prisoners with you, Young Hawk," he said, scowling.

"We were not able to find them, my chief. They have disappeared."

"You rode a large circle?"

"We did. They must have taken horses and ridden toward Fort Zarah."

The chief nodded glumly. "They will bring troops from the fort. It is best we ride now. We will head for Texas. We will leave Kansas completely." Rising, he grunted, "At least we have had vengeance on the cowardly ambushers. Let us go."

Suzanne Lane and Johnny Valentine had been in the hole for over two hours when the thundering of hooves was heard outside the barn. They listened, their hearts pounding, until the sound faded away and all was quiet.

"I think they're gone," Suzanne said optimistically.

"It might be a ruse," Valentine remarked. "We'd better wait a while longer."

When another hour had passed, he lifted up his cramped body and slowly shoved aside the lid. Cautiously he looked around the interior of the barn. All was still. The bodies of Marianna Freeman, Stuart Vance, and Doc Simms were still there. The back door still squeaked and swayed in the late-morning breeze.

Speaking softly, Valentine looked down at Suzanne and said, "You wait here. I'm going to look around. If you hear any gunfire, pull the lid shut."

Scrambling to her feet, the beautiful redhead said, "I'd rather go with you. In fact, I insist on it."

"All right," he said, and he hopped out, reaching down to give her his hand. "Come on. Let's take a look."

Valentine's broken leg felt even stiffer now as he moved carefully toward the front door of the barn, his revolver cocked in his right hand. Suzanne was a few steps behind him, holding her purse tightly in one hand while the other held the .44.

When Valentine first reached the door, he squinted against the painfully bright sunlight, but his eyes quickly adjusted, and he then saw the three fly-covered bodies. Averting his eyes, he looked up to see the cottonwood tree with its rotting bodies of Pearl and Oliver Madison and the blackened, smoldering heaps by the trunk. He felt the gorge rise in his chest, and he thrust a hand behind him to stop Suzanne from going any farther.

"Don't look!" he said. "It's a sight you don't want to see. Let's go out the back door." He holstered his gun and took her by the elbow, hurrying toward the back of the barn.

Suddenly the form of a man standing just inside the back door was silhouetted against the sunlight behind him. Valentine was about to draw when a familiar voice called out.

"Hey, now!" Sid Bingham said gleefully. "Looks like we made it! The Kiowas are gone. I watched 'em ride away across the plains—the whole stinkin' bunch of 'em."

The sensation of danger was pricking at Johnny Valentine's scalp like tiny needles.

There was a wicked leer on the gunfighter's face as he moved forward to meet them. "I managed to climb one of the tall cottonwoods out back," he explained without being asked. "Hid myself way up in the top among the leaves."

Bingham waited for Valentine to say something. They now stood just a few feet apart, but still the taller man made no comment. Suzanne could feel Valentine stiffen, and she watched Bingham carefully, fearful that something was about to happen.

"I heard them two drifters screamin' their lungs out," the gunfighter continued. "Must have been awful, dyin' that way."

Still the man who wore the badge said nothing. Suzanne looked up at him, then back at Bingham once more. She knew the gunfighter was up to something, but she had no idea what it might be. However, something told her that Ford Gunnison knew exactly what it was.

Still leering, Bingham asked, "You two the only ones alive?"

Valentine merely nodded.

"Well, ain't that somethin'. Just us three left." Pausing for effect, he added, "But we can't leave it that way, can we? We can settle it now."

Suzanne felt a cold chill sliver down her spine.

Squinting, the marshal asked, "Settle what?"

"Come now, *Johnny*," Bingham said with a chuckle. "Why do you think I've been hangin' around? I could've left a long time ago."

Valentine's brows had shot up at the name Johnny.

Suzanne thought her ears were playing tricks on her until she saw Valentine's face harden. Perplexed, she looked anxiously between the two men.

"Mrs. Lane is here to witness it," the gunfighter continued, a strange light forming in his eyes. "She can confirm to the world that I outdrew and killed the great Johnny Valentine."

Valentine stared at Bingham, and his heart seemed to stop. The moment had come; the lie was over. How cruelly unfair! He and Suzanne had miraculously survived the harrowing ordeal, but now the love she had for him would turn to hate.

Suzanne's eyes fastened on Valentine's. There was a slight tremor in her voice as she asked, "Ford, what is he talking about? Why is he calling you that?"

Sid Bingham chortled devilishly. "Because that's who he is, pretty lady," he said with a sneer. "I figured it out an hour after we left Dodge."

Suzanne's body froze. What this vile man was saying could not be true. Bolting Bingham with steely, piercing eyes, she rasped, "Johnny Valentine was killed by the Decker gang in Dodge City. I saw his grave."

"I don't know who's in the grave at Dodge, pretty lady," Bingham said flatly, "but it ain't Johnny Valentine. That's him standin' there beside you."

Suzanne's face turned mottled with rage. "You're a liar!"

"Am I? Go ahead and ask him yourself."

Suzanne searched Valentine's eyes. "Ford . . . ?"

The impostor swallowed hard. His voice was thick as he looked away from her gaze and said reluctantly, "He's not lying, Suzanne. I *am* Johnny Valentine."

Suzanne was stunned. Groping for her voice, she asked, "Who . . . who was the man the Decker gang killed in Dodge City?"

"It was my younger brother, Jim. We looked a lot alike. The Decker gang ambushed him, thinking he was me. I arrived in town just after he was gunned down and talked to the undertaker and Doc Simms, explaining that the gang had been after me."

He paused, and Suzanne said nothing. She just stood there staring at him, anger forming in her eyes.

He went on, "I wanted to go after the gang and make them pay for killing my brother. I knew trailing them would be easier if Decker thought I was dead. The town officials all agreed to say the gang had killed me."

"So Doc knew," breathed the redhead.

"Yes."

Suzanne's voice took on a hard edge as she asked, "Where did you get the badge? Did you steal it, too—along with the phony name?"

Valentine explained that U.S. Marshal Ford Gunnison had been in town and was killed along with Jim. "Assuming the marshal's identity and pinning on his badge made it easier to catch Decker and his men."

Looking at him coldly, Suzanne said through her teeth, "So you can murder every member of the gang, too? Like you murdered my husband?"

"Suzanne, I've never murdered anyone!" Valentine retorted. "Frank Lane was going to get his chance to draw!"

Suzanne Lane felt as if she were in some horrid nightmare from which she could not awaken. Her body was suddenly a lifeless thing. She was standing on her feet, but she did not know how, for she was numb all over.

This man, this gunfighter whose only reason for living was to take the lives of other men, had killed her husband. Then he had invaded her world by pretending to be someone else and tricked her into falling in love with him.

*In love with him!* she thought, feeling sick. *How could I have been in love with the man who murdered Frank? I hate him! I hate him!*

Her first impulse was to aim the .44 in her hand at Johnny Valentine and shoot his eyes out. But the cruel despair and disappointment within her surged up and crashed over her like a monstrous wave. Overwhelmed, she turned and put her face against the barn wall, sobbing.

Valentine wanted to run to her, but he knew it was useless. With Suzanne's sobbing tearing at his heart, the tall man looked implacably at the gunfighter and said, "I guess we'd better finish it, Bingham."

Bingham immediately took his stance. "You're known for drawin' with your left. That's a right-hand holster you're wearin'."

"I can draw with either hand the same."

"I thought so," Bingham said evenly.

"That's enough talk. Draw, Bingham. I've got a debt to repay to Doc Simms."

"He had it comin'," Bingham said contemptuously as he took his stance.

Suzanne jerked with a start at the roaring gun. She whirled around. Johnny Valentine was standing with his .45 smoking in his hand. Sid Bingham was lying on his back with a bullet in his heart, his gun still in its holster.

With tears glistening on her face she screamed at Valentine, "It was you! You killed my husband! All the time I thought—" She fought to control her wrath, her eyes ablaze as she struggled to find words to fit what was whirling around in her mind. Too angry to do or say anything else, she turned and leaned against the wall again, burying her face in her arm.

Johnny Valentine ran an uneasy hand across his brow. With his stomach lurching, he came up behind Suzanne as she wept silently. "Suzanne," he said softly, "I've wanted to tell you the truth, but I just didn't know how. You spoke so often about how much you hated the man who killed Frank, even when you thought that man was dead. I knew the moment of truth would have to come sooner or later. I also knew that because of who I am, you and I could never have a life together. But *please*, let me tell you why I was after Frank Lane."

Keeping her back to him, Suzanne listened as Valentine told her the whole story, beginning with Emma's letter. He told of his subsequent run-in with Danny Wellman and Emma's dying in his arms from the stab wounds inflicted by Frank Lane. He ended the story with his pinning on the badge of Marshal Ford Gunnison.

Suzanne bit her lip and said nothing. She knew Valentine was telling the truth about Frank's affair with his sister. Everything fit into place. But her anger was hot, and her pride was injured. Because of his dishonesty, Valentine had been able to take advantage of her. She felt completely humiliated.

Pivoting around suddenly, the redhead glared at him and hissed, "Please, go! Leave me alone!"

Valentine spoke soft and low. "All right, Suzanne, I'll leave you alone. But try to forgive me for deceiving you. I wanted to tell you the truth so bad it was killing me. Instead . . . instead, I kept living a lie, because I knew you would hate me when you learned the truth, and I didn't want to lose you. Suzanne, you must believe me that when I said I had fallen in love with you, I meant it.

And I want you to know something else. When the town council of Dodge City agreed to this plan, they told me that if I was successful, the job of town marshal was mine. I'm going to succeed, Suzanne; I'm going to get Jack Decker. And when I go back to Dodge, I wish somehow I could ask you to go with me as my wife. I love you more than you could ever know, and I always will."

Fixing him with her blazing eyes, Suzanne said hotly, "That's what hurts so bad, Johnny Valentine! I meant it, too, when I said I loved you. But . . . but I had fallen in love with Ford Gunnison. This . . . this is just too much for me to bear. I want you out of my sight right now. I never want to see you again!"

Valentine swallowed hard. "Suzanne, at least let me take you to Great Bend. I want to make sure you get home safely."

"No," she snapped. "I'll get there myself. Go away!"

Johnny Valentine was about to turn and leave when a cold voice coming from the front door cut across the barn.

"He's gonna go away, all right, lady! We're gonna send him to hell right now!"

# Chapter Thirteen

Johnny Valentine tensed as two men came through the door, holding guns on him. The hammers of their revolvers were thumbed back, and by the looks of them these two would think no more of killing a man than of stepping on a cockroach.

The smaller and meaner-looking of the two barked, "Drop your gun to the ground, Valentine!" When Valentine hesitated, the man growled, "Drop it or I'll not only shoot you, but I'll bore a hole in the lady, too!"

Valentine had no doubt he meant it. He carefully removed the .45 from its holster and let it fall to the floor.

"You can drop your gun, too, lady." The man let his gaze wander over her, and he smirked. "After all, a pretty thing like you doesn't have to protect herself. I'd be glad to do it for you."

Suzanne watched fearfully as the unsavory-looking men came closer, and she swallowed hard. She looked at Valentine, then back at the two men. Clearly they were here to kill Johnny Valentine. She hesitated for a moment. Then she dropped the .44 on the ground. "Who are you?" she asked.

The smaller man's mouth cracked into a crooked grin as he said facetiously, "Oh, forgive my rudeness, ma'am! Allow me to introduce us. My name is Nick Hotchkiss. My pal here is Roger Kukar."

"I've never heard of you. What do you want with me?" asked Valentine tartly.

Hotchkiss's grin spread. "We work for Jack Decker. You've heard of *him*, I believe."

Valentine did not answer.

"Well, it don't matter one way or the other. Our orders are to shoot you on sight. Jack will reward us handsomely, and the whole gang will have a celebration while Jack dances on your grave!"

"How did you know I was here?"

Hotchkiss guffawed. "Now that's the real funny part, Valentine. See, we weren't too far out of Dodge after the ambush—in which you *supposedly* died—when Jack got to thinkin' that he wanted to be sure you was dead. I mean, sure we sent a lot of bullets your way—that is, we thought it was you—but Jack, he's the suspicious type, and like I said, he wanted to be sure.

"He sent me back into town to make sure that Johnny Valentine was dead. I figured the best place to do that was the undertakin' parlor. Well, that old undertaker seemed a mite too nervous when I put the question to him. Made *me* suspicious. So with a little . . . *persuadin'*, he told me the truth, includin' how you was masqueradin' as Ford Gunnison and had left town on the stage."

Hotchkiss laughed again and continued, "We'd almost given up hope of ever findin' you, Valentine. When the stage didn't arrive in Great Bend, the officials there figured it must've been attacked by them renegade Kiowas. The clerk at the stage depot told us that a search party was sent out, but all they found was a wreck. No passengers; no bodies. The Army folks thought the Kiowas had captured everyone on the stage and had taken them back to their camp to be tortured."

"But even though you thought the Indians had captured us," Suzanne interrupted, "you still kept up the search? Why?"

"Well, ma'am, Jack don't give up on somethin' when he wants it—and believe me, he wanted Valentine dead *real* bad. Hah! Ol' Jack would've swooped into that renegade camp all by himself, if he'd had to; Valentine was gonna be his. So me and Jack and the boys split up, lookin' all over the territory for them Kiowas. Jack just happened to choose Pawnee Rock as a convenient place for us all to rendez-vous when we was done with our search. Now ain't that somethin'? Wait'll he gets here! He's gonna be a mighty happy man when he sees your body!"

"I guess he's too much of a coward to try and kill me himself."

"Hah!" Hotchkiss declared. "Fact is, Jack's a democratic sort. He figures whoever found you should have the plea-sure of killin' you himself." Looking around the barn, he said mockingly, "And speakin' of killin', you've sure been busy, Valentine. Did you kill all those people out there and the ones in here, too?"

Kukar snarled, "Looks to me like you murdered them just like you murdered Danny Wellman, Valentine. You are one bloody son!"

"And while we're on the subject of relatives, too bad about your brother." Hotchkiss grinned evilly. "Oh, well, you'll be seein' him in a minute. We're sendin' you to meet him—kind of a family reunion."

Valentine knew they would show him no mercy. "At least let the lady go," he said.

Hotchkiss looked back over at Suzanne and slowly ap-praised her. With a toss of his head he said, "All right, sure. I'm feelin' generous, so I'll grant the dyin' man his last wish." With a leer he added, "I'll be catchin' up with you later. I've got better uses for a pretty lady like you. Now, git!"

Suzanne gave Valentine a quick look, and then she hurried past the two outlaws. Hotchkiss watched her with lustful eyes, turning to let his gaze stay on her as she walked through the door.

Valentine knew this was the only chance he would get. With the swiftness of a rattler's tongue he grabbed his gun and fired at Kukar, killing him instantly. But before Valentine's second shot could cut Hotchkiss down, the outlaw spun around and fired, and the slug ripped into Valentine's side. But as he fell he put a bullet through Hotchkiss's heart.

Dropping his revolver, Valentine clutched his bleeding side and rose painfully to his feet. Then he staggered backward several steps and fell again.

Suzanne suddenly appeared at the door and saw that Valentine had been shot. Skirting the two dead outlaws, she walked slowly toward him. She knelt beside him and, in a detached, professional manner, examined his wound.

In an emotionless voice she finally said, "The bullet seems to have gone right through without too much damage. I'm sure you'll survive." She picked up Dr. Simms's medical bag and pulled out a roll of gauze. With sure fingers she had the bandage in place in minutes.

"There," she said, picking up her purse and standing up. "That should hold you for a while. You can fend for yourself from here on. I'm leaving this bloody town. These men have conveniently provided us with saddled horses. I suggest you head for Great Bend and see a doctor. There are several excellent ones there."

Valentine lay there, looking up at her, his heart aching. "Thank you for helping me," he said softly.

She looked at him impassively. Then she turned and walked away.

"I'll always love you, Suzanne!" Valentine called after her.

Suzanne Lane paused a few seconds, not looking back. Then wordlessly she left. He heard her talking reassuringly to one of the horses, and then she mounted up and rode off. The galloping hooves grew ever fainter until the town of Pawnee Rock was once again deathly still.

Johnny Valentine had lain in the same spot for some twenty minutes, the wound in his side giving him much pain. *At least I've been able to forget about my broken leg*, he told himself sardonically. He knew he had to make an attempt to get on his feet and ride out of Pawnee Rock before the rest of the Decker gang showed up.

The horse tied outside suddenly nickered, and seconds later Valentine heard hoofbeats, then male voices. His blood turned to ice. *Decker!* With difficulty he pushed himself to a sitting position, and he was almost overcome with dizziness. He looked around for his gun; it was a good five feet from his reach. From outside the barn he heard one of the outlaws say, "Yep, that's Nick's horse, all right."

The gun seemed a mile away. Gritting his teeth, Valentine began to inch his way toward it.

Three figures suddenly filled the large doorway, outlined distinctly against the brilliant sunlight. "Forget it, Valentine," Jack Decker barked. "Don't even try to reach it." The small man scratched at the patch over his eye. "I knew you'd be here when this thing started throbbin' violently just over the ridge." Spotting his two dead cohorts, Decker growled, "Well, it looks like I owe you for even more now, Valentine! Those were two of my best men!"

Decker drew his gun and moved slowly toward Valentine, showing his slight limp. One man remained near the door, but the other, his bodyguard, Hunt Longley, stayed at Decker's side, towering over him.

The outlaw at the door watched with keen amusement as Decker and Longley advanced on the prostrate man, their revolvers trained on him.

With a wicked glint in his eye Decker said, "Put your gun away, Hunt. This pleasure is gonna be mine. All mine!" Snapping back the hammer of the revolver in his hand, Decker leered demonically at Valentine and hissed, "First, I'm gonna shoot one ear off for Hotchkiss, and then I'll take the other one off for Kukar. And after that, Valentine, you murderous scum, I'm gonna put a bullet between your eyes for my nephew, Danny."

Suddenly a shot racketed through the barn. A bullet tore into the back of Jack Decker's head, dropping the outlaw leader in his tracks.

The outlaw near the door clawed for his gun as he whirled around, but the figure silhouetted in the doorway already had a revolver pointed right between his eyes. Another shot roared, and a black hole appeared right where the gun had been aimed.

Hunt Longley slowly brought his huge, awkward body around and started for the doorway, pulling his gun, but he was too late. The revolver belched fire again. The slug struck Longley in his massive chest, but it did not drop him. Blood spurting from his wound, he howled like an animal and kept going, but the revolver was fired at the giant again, and Longley grunted and jerked from the impact, going down like a felled tree.

Johnny Valentine struggled to a sitting position and squinted through the smoky haze at the person who had saved his life. Stepping from the brilliant sunlight through the doorway, Suzanne Lane stood with her smoking .38 in her hands. Valentine's breath caught in his throat, and his heart started pounding against his rib cage.

Emotionally spent, Suzanne leaned against the doorframe, breathing hard. She opened her hand and let the revolver—which she had orginally put in her purse to use in killing Valentine—drop to the floor. She whisked away the lock of auburn hair that had fallen over her right eye. Turning her head, she looked over at Johnny Valentine and held his eyes with hers for a long moment.

At last she pushed away from the doorframe, slowly walking toward him. As she stood over him tears glistened in her eyes, spilling onto her cheeks. She did not bother to wipe them away.

"I had to come back," she said softly.

Valentine looked up at her quizzically.

Her full lips curved into a sweet smile. "Dodge City's new marshal really ought to have a wife."

# THE BADGE

### Book 8
## THE STRANGER
*by Bill Reno*

When a wounded man awakes in a Utah cemetery with no memory, a struggle to learn the truth begins. The bloody bodies of three hardcases also lie above ground in the cemetery, and the amnesia victim has no way of knowing whether they were his opponents or allies. Two townsmen and their beautiful sister, Bonnie, find the wounded stranger and take him to Green River's physician. While he recovers, John Stranger, as he comes to be known, becomes a suspect in a bank robbery perpetrated by the three dead men at the cemetery. But he also becomes an important part of Bonnie Bodine's life, and though no one can account for Stranger's past, she feels certain that he is innocent.

At the same time, Sam Bodine, the oldest brother of the Bodine clan and the town's marshal, is found brutally murdered, and soon a prominent businessman turns up dead. It becomes clear that a murderer is on the loose, and John Stranger, as he searches for clues to his identity, is drawn into the investigation. But as more bodies are found, a chilling mystery threatens to send Green River's citizens into a mindless frenzy—unless John Stranger can use his natural powers of leadership and persuasion to stop them.

Read **THE STRANGER**, on sale December 1988 wherever Bantam paperbacks are sold.

U.S. MARSHAL

From the creators of the exciting
STAGECOACH series comes

## THE BADGE
### by Bill Reno

To a violent land, a frontier yet untamed, came a man who wore the badge of law and order. He faced the myriad dangers and paid the price in blood to become one of the most enduring heroic figures of the Old West.

#1: SUNDANCE (26774-4 • $2.95)
#2: THE FACELESS MAN (26785-X • $2.95)
#3: BLACK COFFIN (26997-6 • $2.95)
#4: POWDER RIVER (27118-0 • $2.95)
#5: LONDON'S REVENGE (27217-9 • $2.95)
#6: THE SHOWDOWN (27349-3 • $2.95)
#7: THE IMPOSTER (27466-X • $2.95)

and coming in December 1988, #8: THE STRANGER

✦ ★ BADGE ★ ✦

- - - - - - - - - - - - - - - - - - - - - - - - - - - - -